A King Production presents…

A New Beginning

A Novel

DEJA KING

This novel is a work of fiction. Any references to real people, events, establishments, or locales are intended only to give the fiction a sense of reality and authenticity. Other names, characters, and incidents occurring in the work are either the product of the author's imagination or are used fictitiously, as those fictionalized events and incidents that involve real persons. Any character that happens to share the name of a person who is an acquaintance of the author, past or present, is purely coincidental and is in no way intended to be an actual account involving that person.

ISBN 13: 978-0-98433257-1
ISBN 10: 098433257X
Cover concept by Joy Deja King & www.MarionDesigns.com
Cover layout and graphic design by: www.MarionDesigns.com
Cover model: Deja King
Typesetting: Marion Designs
Editor: Suzy McGlown and Linda Williams

Library of Congress Cataloging-in-Publication Data;
King, Deja

Bitch A New Beginning: a novel by Deja King
For complete Library of Congress Copyright info visit;
www.dejaking.com

A King Production
P.O. Box 912, Collierville, TN 38027

A King Production and the above portrayal log are trademarks of A King Production LLC

Printed in Canada

Acknowledgements

I want to thank all my loyal readers and the people who continue to support me. I've been on such a long fulfilling journey since getting my first publishing deal in 2005 and my first novel being published in 2006. With all that I've been through, the good, the bad and the ugly I have no regrets. I feel blessed and honored to have the most amazing fan base ever and a loyal team that understands my vision for A King Production. You, my readers' show me so much unconditional love that in those moments in my career where I've almost felt defeated, you all gave me the strength and determination to not give up. THANK YOU for that!

As I start a new phase in my career with publishing my first author I hope you all continue to support me in this journey. I also pray that you all enjoy my newest production, Bitch A New Beginning as this series means a great deal to me. I so don't want to let you all down as I know many of you have been anticipating the release of this novel. I hope you believe that I've done these characters justice as they hold a special place in my heart as you my readers do also. I LOVE you all so much never doubt that. Please hit me up on Twitter for your feedback @ joydejaking. Hugs and Kisses ☺

This Book is Dedicated To My:

Family, Readers and Supporters.
I LOVE you guys so much. Please believe that!!

Preface

The Present...

Ring...ring...ring

"Hello."

"Mommy, it's me, Aaliyah." Precious glanced over at the clock to see what time it was.

"Where are you and why are you calling so late?" Precious wanted to know trying to snap out of her sleep.

"I've gotten myself in a bit of a situation."

"What sort of situation? And where are Amir and Justina? I thought you were supposed to be with them tonight?"

"I am...I mean I was but something came up."

"Cut the bullshit, Aaliyah. What the hell is going on?"

"I'm in jail and I need you to come get me out."

"Jail!" Precious screamed it out so loud that it awoke Supreme from his sleep. "You're in jail!"

"Yes. And could you please not yell. I already have a migraine headache as it is."

"Aaliyah, what are they charging you with?" Precious asked. She gripped the phone trying to stop herself from wanting to reach through it and snatch her daughter up.

"First Degree Murder."

Aaliyah

Mother/Daughter
Born This Way

The Past...

My mother came from nothing but was determined to have it all. I was born having it all but wanted more. So in reality mother and daughter were exactly alike or at least I thought so. See in my eyes, my mother was a Boss Bitch. From the time I was a little girl I admired everything about her and knew when I grew up I would be her. For those that don't know, my mother is the one and only Precious Cummings Mills and I am her daughter, Aaliyah Mills Carter.

Unlike my mother who was born and raised in the grimiest Brooklyn projects, I grew up in the opulent world of Beverly Hills. The closest I got to Brooklyn was the Upper East Side in Manhattan. You would think with the vast difference in our upbringing that our personalities would be polar opposite but that couldn't have been further from the truth. Although I was born with a silver spoon in my mouth I inherited the fire that would forever brew inside my mother. That trait we shared was made evident at my eleventh birthday party. As I sat in my holding cell I thought back to that day, seven years ago.

"Aaliyah, come on! Everybody is waiting for you to open your birthday presents."

"They have to wait. I need to change my outfit."

"What's wrong with the outfit you have on?"

"This was my introduction dress now we're moving on to part two. I have to give my guest another look," I explained taking off my pretty in pink silk sleeveless dress with draped ruffles curving down the front. The dress screamed 'princess' but now I wanted to put on something that yelled out 'it girl'. I couldn't wait to put on the silver and black romper that was artfully embellished with metal studs down the front and around the neckline.

"Where did you get that from?" my mother barked standing in front of me.

"Daddy got it."

"I know Supreme didn't get that."

"No not that daddy, my other daddy, Nico." I watched my mother's face quickly frown up. Even while angry she was still the most beautiful woman in the world to me. She didn't say anything for a few minutes and I was afraid she was going to demand I take off the romper I had been dreaming about wearing since my dad got it for me a week ago. He had this lady that custom designed clothes for celebrity kids make it for me.

"Only because it's your birthday am I going to let you wear that grown outfit but it's a onetime thing."

"Thank you, mommy," I smiled wrapping my arms around her tiny waist. As I held her tightly I wondered when I got older and had a couple of kids would I still look that good. Her chain-stripe print dress with a tassel-tie waist and layered hemline highlighted her figure perfectly without overexposure.

"How can I look in those eyes and deny my baby girl."

"Mommy, daddy said bring Aaliyah to open her presents."

"Here we come, Xavier. We can all go down together."

"Mom, I don't want to go back out there escorted by my mom and little brother. You all go first and I'll be right behind you to make my entrance."

"Girl you a mess," my mom laughed, "Just like I was. We won't stop you from making your entrance," she continued as she took my five-year-old brother's hand and walked out.

I twirled around one more time in the mirror and hurried out. I was anxious for all my friends to see me in my specially designed just for me outfit. When I stepped out into the lavishly decorated courtyard I was devastated when I didn't see a crowd of well-wishers waiting patiently for my entrance. Instead everybody was gathered around the waterfall. I started walking towards the commotion when Justina and Amir approached me.

"Aaliyah, you don't need to go over there," Justina said grabbing my arm.

"And why not?" I asked yanking my arm out of her grasp.

"Because my dad said they were over there handling grown folk business and we needed to stay out the way."

"Well T-Roc ain't my daddy! So you stay right here, I'm going over there."

"Aaliyah, I really think you should listen to Justina," Amir added.

"Justina doesn't run me! This is *my* birthday party," I stressed. As I hurried forward, from the corner of my eye I could see Justina and Amir trailing right behind me. I began carefully maneuvering my way through the crowd of adults hoping not to get noticed by my parents or grandfather. As I got closer I could hear what sounded like my mother raising her voice and my dad trying to calm her down. When I got to the forefront I could see my dad holding my mother back and I immediately ran by her side to see what had her so upset.

"Mommy, what's wrong?"

"Supreme, let me go! I don't need you holding my arms like I'm some uncontrollable child!"

"But you are out of control right now. You can't get to fighting up in here. Think about Aaliyah and Xavier."

"They'll understand!" my mom growled. I could tell the claws were about to come out.

"Mommy, mommy, what happened?" This time I screamed out desperate to get her attention. When she finally met my stare, my mother could see the tears swelling up in my eyes.

My dad let her arms go and she cupped my face in her hands. "I'm so sorry, Aaliyah. Please don't cry."

"Why are you upset?"

"It's nothing you need to worry yourself about, it..."

"Look at my beautiful niece," I heard a female voice say interrupting my mother. I turned my head around and noticed a familiar face that I hadn't seen in years.

"Maya, what are you doing here?"

"That's Aunt Maya," she smiled. She stepped near me and my Grandpa Quentin quickly pulled her back.

"Don't you dare speak to my daughter! You 'bout to regret that you ever stepped foot in this birthday party!" My mother was ready to step out her open-toe stilettos and jump on Maya in front of everybody. I knew my mother could get upset because occasionally I would hear her arguing with my dad but never did I see her like this. She seemed ready for war.

"All I came to do was wish my niece a happy birthday and give her a present. I haven't seen her since I first came home."

"You mean since you got out of jail, you psychopath!"

"Precious, calm down."

"Don't tell me to calm down. She probably found out about this party through you. You know how I feel about her! You've made it clear that you embrace her as your daughter but that heffa ain't no sister of mine. And once I drag her ass up outta here she'll learn not to listen to what you say when it comes to me!" Right

7

before my mother lunged at Maya my dad grabbed her again.

"Listen, if you put your hands on her she might try to press charges or some dumb shit like that," I heard my dad trying to whisper in my mom's ear. "Think about the kids, she ain't worth going to jail over. Instead let's lock her up for trespassing."

"I don't want to cause any problems. Here, Aaliyah, take my present and then I'll leave," Maya offered as if she heard what my father was planning to do. I walked towards Maya and my mom reached out to grab me but I turned around and smiled before continuing on my way.

"Let the child take the present," my Grandpa Quentin suggested wanting to be the peacemaker.

"Here's a beautiful present for such a beautiful girl," Maya said bending over to hand me over a small Tiffany box with a white ribbon. With one hand I took the present and with the other hand I swung it back as far as I could and slapped her face so hard that my hand was hurting.

"That's for disrespecting my mommy," I belted after my hand left an imprint on her face. "And this is for ruining my birthday party," I screamed out again, tossing the Tiffany box she just gave me in her face.

Everybody went silent and Maya stared at me as if in complete shock. I stared her back down daring her to even look as if she wanted to slap me back. She and I both knew that everybody in this party would jump on her if it even appeared she had any intentions of doing that.

"I think it's best you leave," my Grandpa Quentin

finally said, breaking the silence.

"Yes, Grandpa, I agree with you," I said before turning back to Maya. "You need to leave and don't ever come back. You're not welcome in this family." I walked back over to my mother and stood by her side. "I love you, mommy."

"I love you too, Aaliyah."

Amir

FATHER/SON
Groomed This Way

My father taught me at a young age that it's not what you do but how you do it. My dad is Genesis and his persona reflects the same power as his name. From the moment my dad started to allow me to really be around him in not only his personal dealings but business I wanted to follow in his footsteps. But he always reiterated that I should study what he did and learn how to do it better. That kind of bothered me because I didn't think it could get any better than him. He seemed to provide it all and then some. We lived extremely well but he made it clear that if I worked hard I could live even greater. Growing up I didn't know how much greater it could get. We had a palatial penthouse in Philly and another in New Jersey and New York since he did a lot of business with Nico Carter. Nico lived in a crazy mansion in Alpine, NJ. We could've easily had one too but my dad said we were bachelors and bachelors didn't need all that space because it would turn into another unnecessary headache.

With all that we had, the one thing missing was my mother. I never knew her as my dad explained she was murdered while pregnant with me...she died but yet I somehow lived. That sometimes haunted me and for a long time it haunted my father. I think that was one of the reasons it took him so long to include me in his life. For most of my younger years I remembered first spending the majority of time with a woman named CoCo, who one day just stopped coming around. When I asked my dad what happened to her he simply said she went away and I left it at that. I later found out there was much more to that story. After that I basically had nannies and my Aunt Nichelle who became like a mother to me. But that couldn't replace the void I knew my father had. He would never admit to it but I felt it was there. Mainly because he always stressed to me how important it was that I find my soul mate, get married and raise a family. If he wanted that for me then he had to want it for himself. My father understood how being in love could lift you up but losing it could also tear you apart. That became obvious to me a year earlier when a business associate and friend came to visit my dad after getting out of jail wanting his help.

As I sat in my car outside the police station waiting for my dad, Nico, Precious and Supreme to arrive to try and get Aaliyah out of jail, I thought how that visit from my dad's friend a year ago seemed like yesterday. At that time I had no idea the impact his friend would have on each of us. His visit seemed to redefine all of our lives.

"Dad, we need to be heading out in a little while. We don't want to be late for the game."

"What game?"

"Knicks...Lakers. We've been talking about it for the last month."

"Damn, I forgot about that. I can't go."

"What! Why not?"

"Someone is coming over to discuss something important with me."

"Someone like who? And they're important enough to miss this big game for?"

"You don't know him, Amir, but yes he is important. Not only do we do business together but I also consider him a friend." Hearing the word friend come out my dad's mouth instantly got my attention and piqued my interest since I rarely heard my father ever refer to someone as a friend. When he would reminisce about some of the fun times while on the come up, he always mentioned who he considered his best friend and brother, Deuce. I knew he considered Nico, T-Roc and Quentin to be close friends. So I was dying to know who this mystery person was he felt was important enough to miss the game over.

"I understand."

"I appreciate that. But you go 'head to the game. Take one of your friends."

"That's okay. I have some studying I need to catch up on anyway."

"Are you sure? I know how much you were looking forward to going," he said giving me a peculiar look.

"Yeah, I'm sure. They'll be other games."

"You know I'm never gonna stop you from studying."

And that was the exact reason I used studying as my excuse to stay home. One thing about my dad, he always emphasized the importance of an education. Even though he figured out how to make millions and millions of dollars with only a GED to his name and never stepping foot in a university he told me that striving for a great education was the best gift I could ever give him.

"I know dad," I laughed before hearing the doorbell. "That must be your friend now."

"Let me introduce you to him before you go study."

"Sure," I grinned. Knowing the only reason I was skipping the game was to see who this friend was. I could hear my dad talking as he was walking back down the hallway towards me.

"Amir, this is Lorenzo. Lorenzo, this is my son." He gave me a firm shake.

"He's a handsome young man. You should be proud, Genesis."

"I am and he's smart too," my dad beamed making me feel extra good about myself.

"It was nice meeting you, Lorenzo. I'm going to do some studying now." I headed in the direction of my bedroom waiting until I heard my father close the door to his office before I turned around. I stood for a few minutes and then slightly cracked the door open so I could hear what they were discussing. From the looks of Lorenzo I knew my dad wasn't exaggerating when he said what they had to discuss was important. Lorenzo had important written all over him. He had a commanding presence much like my father. And although he had on some simple black pants and black shirt, the fabric and fit was meticulous as if tailored made.

"Man, I'm so glad you're out of jail. I hated not being able to come see you but I stayed in constant touch with your attorneys."

"Genesis, we both know how the game go. When somebody's hot you stay the fuck away. No sense in us both being locked up. Then who's on the outside to help."

"I'm just glad you're here and you look good. I see those few months behind bars didn't put a dent in your swagger."

"No, but it did put a dent in my heart."

"Huh?" I could hear in the tone of my dad's voice he wasn't expecting Lorenzo to say that. I saw him hand Lorenzo a drink before continuing. "A dent in your heart, I had no idea you were that serious with somebody. What happened, she couldn't handle things when you got locked up and bailed on you?"

"It would appear that way but I think it's something else."

"I'm not following you."

"When I got locked up she couldn't handle being out there in that entertainment industry without me supporting her mentally so she turned back to her old habits which were drugs. Supposedly it became too much for her and she died of an overdose."

"You say supposedly, you don't believe that's what happened?"

"My gut is telling me no. I mean I believe drugs were involved but I think somebody wanted to make it look like it was an overdose but some shady shit actually went down."

"You mean like somebody murdered her?"

"Exactly."

"Do you know who the person is that you think is responsible."

"Yes, Sway Stone."

The Sway Stone, I was about to ask out loud but caught myself and put my hand over my mouth. But then I heard my dad ask for me.

"Sway Stone, the rapper?"

"Yeah, that muthafucka."

"How did the woman know Sway?"

"They dated for a while before we got together." My dad started scratching his head and I did too. It was a natural habit we both had when we were thinking hard about something. I assumed he was trying to figure out who this woman was because that was exactly what I was trying to do.

"The young lady that died not too long ago, she was a reality star...right?"

"Yes."

"When she died she was in all the papers and on a few news programs. Was she the one he got arrested for beating up at a hotel?"

"You seem to know everything going on in pop culture."

"It comes with having a teenage son."

"But yes, her name was Dior."

"I had no idea you all were together. But then how would I, we rarely saw each other. I guess that's how you know that you're close to somebody. You don't see them often but when they need you, you're there."

"And that's why I'm here tonight because I need you, Genesis."

"Whatever you need I got you."

"Even though my attorney was able to get the charges the Feds had against me thrown out for lack of evidence, I know they're still trying to build a case. So I have to lay low and be super clean for the next few months. I mean I'm not even trying to get a speeding ticket."

"That's smart."

"But I need to get to Sway and I know you have connections in the music industry. So do I but again, I'm laying low and I don't trust any of the people that I associate with in that business to keep my shit confidential. But I know you will and that's why I trust you."

"Are you saying that you want to have Sway Stone killed?"

"If I find out that he had anything to do with Dior's death, that's exactly what I want."

"Say, you're right. How do we even get him to admit some shit like that?"

"Sway is a straight up functioning junky. He stays high off something. And he love to get fucked up with women, lots of women. I know this young lady that has that groupie party girl look and is familiar with him who just needs the proper introduction to infiltrate his circle. Once she's in, I'm positive if she asks him the right questions while he's fucked up he'll come clean. His ego gets off on bullshit like that."

"I can make that happen. But what if we find out he had nothing to do with it?"

"Then let him live but I know he did. I'll be the first to admit that Dior had a problem with drugs. But the last time I saw her when she came to visit me in jail, I could tell she was hurt but at the same time she was holding strong. I promised her I would beat the case and come back to her and when I looked in her eyes she believed me. Maybe I'm wrong but I don't believe she went home and decided to get high. Dior understood that I couldn't be with a woman who was a junkie. Especially..." I heard a break in Lorenzo's voice.

"You were going to say, especially because of the situation with your mom." My dad said finishing Lorenzo's sentence.

"Exactly. Dior had been doing so well fighting off those demons I don't believe she had a relapse. I'm in the business we both are so I know how this addiction thing go. But a lot of time users have given up on life and don't feel like they have anything to live for but a high; it wasn't like that for Dior. We were going to get married, start a life together. She was the only woman I ever saw myself being able to do that with and to have her taken away from me. Beyond all that, you know how you get this feeling in your gut about something that you can't shake."

"I know the feeling you're talking about."

"Well that's the feeling I have about Sway Stone. On everything I believe I know he had something to do with Dior's death."

"When Talisa was murdered although I couldn't

prove it at the time I knew Arnez was behind it. And I wasn't going to leave this earth until I knew for a fact he was no longer walking it."

"Then you understand how I feel about Sway."

"Completely. It's like your heart has been ripped out, and although you can never put it back together, knowing you sought vengeance against the person responsible makes you sleep a little easier at night."

"Exactly. Once the person responsible for Dior's death is dead and gone I will sleep a little easier at night. And while you're working on that I'm making sure Alexus and Lala are found and dealt with accordingly too."

"I still can't believe Alexus turned on you. She seemed so loyal. What am I talking about, CoCo was my Alexus. Luckily for you, you weren't fuckin' Alexus or were you?"

"No we never crossed that line but it didn't stop her from turning on me."

"Trust me, if you had been sleeping with her then the betrayal would've felt ten times worse. I was engaged and going to marry CoCo. I let her be a mother to my son when she was partly responsible for taking his mom away from him in the first place."

A painful knot in my stomach hit me when I heard what my father said. I always wondered why CoCo vanished out of our lives and now I knew. I also understood why my father had no interest in settling down during all these years because there was no way he could trust women. I decided that I heard enough.

My mind was already going in circles hearing that my favorite rapper was not only a drug addict but there was a good chance he played a role in the death of his ex-girlfriend. I also was processing that if Sway Stone ended up dead more than likely my father had something to do with it. But what had thrown me most off balance was finding out that the woman my dad had planned on spending the rest of his life with was responsible for almost single handily destroying both father and son.

Aaliyah

BFF
(Best Friends Forever)

When I stared around the four walls holding me captive I kept wondering how I got here. It amazed me how quickly my life had changed in less than twenty-four hours. What started off as being the best summer of my life had now become my worst nightmare. Instead of preparing to go off to college I was facing a life in prison with no chance of parole. *How could that be* I thought to myself. This summer started off like all the others had been for the last several years, spending it with Justina and Amir. The three of us were like a clique and being together during the summer was a ritual.

In the early years Justina and Amir spent more time together because they both went to school on the east coast. But right when Justina was about to begin high school her dad T-Roc decided to maintain most of his business on the west coast so we ended up attending the same prep school in Beverly Hills. We were always close but when Justina started attending my school that's when our bond was solidified. I remember the day she knew I would always have her back.

"That must be the new girl. Look at her, she has no style. And check out that bun, what is she supposed to be a librarian," the girls laughed loudly. They continued on with their slick talking not knowing I was right behind them listening to it all. They were standing several feet away from Justina watching her as she was getting her books out her locker.

"We should bump into her and make her drop all her books." One girl suggested.

"Yeah, that would be hilarious! You go first, and then when she's trying to pick her stuff up we'll knock her back down."

"Cool come on!" They picked up their speed as Justina was closing her locker shut.

"I wouldn't do that if I was you," I screamed out as they got to the halfway point." All three of the catty girls turned around at the same time to see who was interrupting their little plot.

"Hey, Aaliyah! You must want in on our little joke," they giggled. When Justina heard them call out my name she stopped what she was doing and turned in my direction.

"No, I don't want in on your little joke," I made that clear when I got right up on the girls. They looked at each other baffled. I guess they assumed because we were on the cheerleading squad together I was one of them.

"Then what is it because we're about to go have some fun with the new girl."

"Justina, come here." Justina looked down at the hallway floor for a second then walked over. "Listen, this is my best friend Justina," I said holding her hand.

"You know her?" one of them asked with an attitude.

"Didn't I just say she's my best friend you idiot."

"Now you're calling me an idiot, she's the idiot, look at her," they all burst out laughing.

"I'm only going to say this once you stuck up bitches. If any of you so much as breathe in her direction you're going to have to deal with me and I promise none of you want that."

"Are you threatening us because I'll report you," the Miley Cyrus lookalike warned.

"Will that be before or after I mop this floor with your face?"

"Come on girls, let's go," she huffed as they stormed off.

"That was classic, Aaliyah," Justina finally said letting out a huge laugh.

"Well they had it coming."

"You didn't have to do that for me."

"Yes I did! We've been down since hopscotch and hula hoops. Did you really think I was going to let some Paris Hilton knockoffs disrespect you? Please! Now come on, I'll walk you to your next class."

From that day forward Justina and I were inseparable. It gave Justina confidence to know that she wasn't alone in her new school and that if we didn't have anybody else we had each other. I eventually even quit the cheerleading squad because at every practice I was a step away from beating one of those dizzy broads down. I didn't need them anyway, I had Justina.

When I got home from school that day I was looking forward to telling my mother what happened. She got a kick hearing about the mindless socialites in training I went to school with. But instead of having the chance to share in my high school melodrama I was greeted by another heated argument between my mom and dad. They were so loud they didn't even hear me call out to them when I came inside. Of course my curiosity got the best of me. Instead of going upstairs, shutting my door and blasting my music so I could drown out their voices I stood by the living room so I could hear exactly what they were saying.

"Aren't you sick and tired of arguing about the same bullshit all the time because I know I am!"

"What do you expect when you have a child by another man that was conceived during our marriage and you constantly stay in contact with?"

"How many times do I have to say this, I thought you were dead! And of course we have to stay in contact we have a daughter together. What, am I not supposed to have a conversation with the father of my child?"

"You just don't get it."

"No, I don't, Supreme. I gave you a son. What more do you want from me?"

"Oh, you gave me a son. You make it sound like Xavier was some consolation prize for taking away a daughter that was supposed to be mine."

"I've ran out of things to say to explain myself to you. You constantly throw Nico in my face yet you slept with that sick, twisted and deranged Maya. I've learned to forgive you for that but Nico is constantly the fuckin' elephant in the room."

"I'll never forgive myself for falling for Maya's lies but I have no dealings with her. The way you carry on with Nico you're continuously throwing that shit in my face. I mean are you going to be doing this until Aaliyah is a senior citizen."

"We're friends and we're parents what am I supposed to do?"

"Make a choice."

"I did! I chose you. I chose our family."

"Then why hasn't Nico ever gotten married. Does he even have a woman in his life that he's dating seriously? No!"

"How do you know?"

"Because if he did, she wouldn't allow him to be on the phone all the time running his mouth to you!"

"There's nothing going on between me and Nico."

"Maybe not physically but definitely mentally. You may not want to admit it to yourself but it's true. You all are having an emotional affair which can be more dangerous to a marriage than a physical one."

"We have to talk about this later. I need to go pick up Xavier."

I quickly ran upstairs to my bedroom when I heard my mother say that. I flopped down on the bed and stared up at the ceiling. I now regretted letting my curiosity get the best of me. It wasn't meant for me to hear all the awful things they said to each other. My mother had told me about some of the heinous things Maya had did when I was a little girl, like having me kidnapped and holding my mother hostage but I never knew she slept with my dad. I also thought that my mom got pregnant with me before she married my dad, not during the marriage. Now I understood why for all these years there were occasional fireworks going off in the Mills household that seemed to be more frequent in recent months.

The happiest my parents seemed to be was when my mom was pregnant with Xavier and the first few years after he was born. My dad practically worshipped my mom. He wouldn't let her lift a finger to do a thing. Not only did I have a nanny but during her pregnancy he made sure my mom had her own personal assistant to cater to her every need. Whether it was cooking, shopping, running her bath water, you name it the assistant had to do it. He didn't want my mom to stress over anything. Then it seemed every other day he was bringing her home some sort of gift and I'm not talking flimsy stuff. I'm talking cars, diamonds and furs—mind you, it didn't even get that cold in LA. My dad just simply adored my mother and he wanted her to have everything he thought she might want. I remembered hoping and praying that I would find a guy who would love me half as much as my dad loved my mom.

"Aaliyah, are you home?" I heard my mom ask as she knocked on my bedroom door.

"Yes, I'm here," I called out.

"I'm about to pick up your brother do you want to ride with me?"

"No thanks."

"Are you sure?"

"Yes, I'm tired. I had a long day at school."

"Ok, get some rest. I'll see you when we get back."

"Ok." Normally I would jump at the chance to go riding with my mom to pick up my little brother. Having our chats in the car was a highlight of my day, something I looked forward to but not today. There was no hiding the gloom on my face and my mother would want to know what was wrong with me. I wasn't ready to discuss with her all that I heard. I was still dealing with it myself. Right now all I wanted to do was close my eyes and pretend just for a little while that everything in the Mills' household was bliss.

Amir

Can't Break The Chain

My patience was getting the best of me waiting for my dad and Aaliyah's family to get here. I knew she was going crazy being locked up like an animal. I was losing my mind wanting answers. All I knew is what Aaliyah told me before I'm assuming the cops took her cell phone. She called me in a panic saying she was about to get arrested for murder and the phone went dead. I tried calling her back but her cell had been turned off. I was blowing up Justina's phone to find out if she knew anything but it kept going straight to voicemail.

"Justina where are you?" I mumbled out loud as I grew more and more frustrated. I slumped back in the car seat and closed my eyes trying to calm my nerves. I began reflecting back to what could've led to this moment right now.

"Dad, can I get...oh I didn't realize you had

company," I said standing in the doorway of my dad's office with three set of eyes all on me.

"You know I'm not company," Nico smiled, trying to ease an uncomfortable situation. My dad seemed in a fucked up mood which made me nervous and Nico could probably sense that.

"Amir, I'm in the middle of a meeting with Nico and Lorenzo. Whatever you need will have to wait."

"Maybe I can help. Do you mind if I sit in on the meeting?" I tried to make the suggestion casually but in a firm tone so that my dad could tell I was serious. I was seventeen now and more and more each day I was feeling like a man and I wanted to be a part of the empire my dad had built.

"Son, if you want to help me, then you'll close the door and not interrupt me until I've finished handling my business."

"Come on, Genesis. Let the young man have a seat. We started making moves at a lot younger age than him. He needs to learn from the best." My dad glared at Nico not amused by what he suggested. Lorenzo remained silent in the cut drinking what appeared to be a glass of Ace of Spades.

"Dad, I promise to be quiet and just listen."

"What can it hurt, Genesis, and I don't have a problem with it, do you, Lorenzo?"

"That's Genesis's son, the only opinion that matters is his."

"Like I said, Amir, please excuse yourself. I'll get with you when I'm done."

"I understand. I'll be in my room," I lied before

closing the door. I had no intentions of going anywhere but right where I was at so I could eavesdrop on their meeting. I found myself doing that a lot lately but it was because my dad wasn't leaving me a choice. His life and what he did intrigued me but my dad would never let me in. No matter how many times I asked him to show me how his business operations worked he seemed to find a way to shut it down. Normally it would be subtle but tonight was different. He appeared agitated and was direct with me about leaving him alone. All that did was make me more curious. I was listening so hard my ears felt like they were on fire.

"Nico, I would appreciate if you don't ever do that again."

"Genesis, it was a joke."

"Joke? We dealing with a snake ass nigga who has the potential to cost us millions and millions of dollars and you want to use a word like joke. The only joke you need to concern yourself with is the one that's gonna be on us if we don't find a way to eliminate our problem."

"I feel you but we'll find a way, we always do. But real talk, I do think you need to start bringing Amir in the fold. He's a mature young man that will more than likely run your business one day."

"Not if I have anything to do with it."

"Genesis, you can't be serious? That's your son. I wish I had a son to bring into the loop and run my shit."

"I want better for my son. This isn't the life for him."

"Maybe you should let him decide that."

"Lorenzo, didn't you just say my opinion was the only one that mattered when it came to my son?"

"Yes and that's true. But as your son gets older he has the right to decide what he wants out of life too. You say you want better for him but to Amir it may not get no better than this. The same way the blood of a hustler runs through you, your son might have inherited it too. And just like you can't be denied, neither can he."

"Fuck that! My son will run an empire but it will be one you can find on the Forbes List."

"I hear you, man. But if Amir steps to you with something different don't turn him away. You can't fault him for wanting to follow in his father's footsteps."

"Nico, I know what's best for my son...hold up, this the call I've been waiting on," I heard my father say. My ear was pressed so hard against the door I was afraid I would knock it down. I couldn't really make out what he was saying during the phone call but whatever it was his words were short and to the point.

"So what did he say?"

"Let's go. He got him at our warehouse in Brooklyn."

"I'll have Dice bring the car around."

"Cool, then I'll ride with you, Genesis."

"We can all ride together," I heard Nico say. I heard scrambling as if everybody was getting their stuff together to break out so I bolted to my room. I turned my music on and the television so when my dad came to say goodbye I would seem like I had been doing my own thing.

Five minutes went by, then ten and when it hit fifteen I came out my room to see what was going on. "Dad," I called out and got no response. After doing a walkthrough of the penthouse I realized they had all left. For my dad to bounce without saying goodbye I knew what was going on had to be critical and I needed to find out what it was. I had been to the warehouse in Brooklyn a few times so I knew its exact location. I grabbed my car keys and headed out the door.

As I was pulling off the Brooklyn Bridge and turning to get on Flatbush I heard my cell ringing. I looked down and saw it was Aaliyah and ignored it but she kept calling back. After the fourth time she called I finally picked up.

"What is it?" I said abruptly.

"Wow, is that anyway to greet your best friend."

"I'm in the middle of something," I sulked.

"What, fuckin'? I mean what else would have you so pissy for me interrupting you."

"Aaliyah, shut the hell up. What is it?"

"I was only kidding! What's your problem?"

"You at the moment. I told you I'm busy. You blowing up my phone like there is some sort of emergency. So what is it?"

"I wanted to talk to you about this guy I met."

"You blowing up my phone over some dude!"

"Oh, like you ain't never discussed a chick with me before."

"That ain't the point. Listen, I don't have time for this right now, Aaliyah. I'll call you later." I ended the call without even giving her a chance to respond. Aaliyah could be draining and right now I didn't have the energy to give her. All I was focused on was playing detective.

When I pulled up to the warehouse I noticed

two black Suburban's and my dad's charcoal Maybach. I pulled slightly in then put my Range in reverse and decided to drive a few blocks up and park on the side of the street. I went around the back way because I knew my dad kept a security camera in the front so they could capture all the activity. I used the set of keys my dad gave me to open the back door. I remembered when he gave them to me. He stated I should only use them if something happened to him and if it did, specific instructions were left for me on how to proceed.

Of course I knew that wasn't the current circumstances but I had to know what was going on with my dad. He would only give me a glimpse of the life he lived and I wanted to see it all. I felt I no longer needed to be protected. I was becoming a man and it was time he let me fully be part of his business operations. I guess you could say I was forcing the issue or better yet forcing my way in.

I opened and closed the back door as quietly as I could but it wouldn't have mattered. There was so much chaos going on, nobody could've heard me regardless.

"Motherfucker, you betta tell us who the fuck you working for. And I want government names not no street alias shit!" I heard my dad say in a loud yet calm tone.

"Man, I already told you that all I know is he go by the name of Dale."

"Nigga, please! You been working with this motherfucker for the last couple months and all you got for us is Dale. You must think we some dummies. Genesis, told you he want a government name and that's what the fuck he meant." I wasn't sure but that sounded like Nico talking and I was dying to know who had them so fucking pissed off. There was a short hallway that led to the massive opening of the warehouse. I tried to maneuver my way against the wall so I could see out but nobody could see me. Luckily where I was standing was dark but a few feet away the light was bright.

"I don't know what ya'll want from me. I told you everything I know. I swear I didn't have a clue that nigga was the enemy. I thought he was tryna do straight up legitimate business, not no bullshit."

"Is that right, Tony?"

"Yeah, Genesis, I swear! It wasn't until you sent your men to snatch me up that I realized there was trouble. Before that I thought I was one of your best workers."

"I tell you what. You want to prove your worth?"

"No doubt, man. I need you to know that I'm down for you and nobody else."

"Cool. Here's your phone. Call this nigga Dale and tell him you need to see him immediately."

"Ahh, umm, well," I heard the dude stuttering.

"What's the problem, Tony? You said you wanted to prove your worth so get to dialing the number."

"The thing is, I don't ever call him. He always call me from a private number."

"Is that right."

"Yeah. I thought that shit was a little odd but now I understand why he was doing it. He was protecting himself in case his cover got blown."

"You seem to have it all figured out, Tony."

"I'm telling you the truth."

"Genesis, this bum ass nigga ain't gon' tell us shit.

He's wasting our fuckin' time."

"Lorenzo, I think you might be right."

"No he ain't, Genesis! I swear man, I'm on your side. I had no idea that nigga was tryna take over your drug operation. All he said was that he wanted in on the action. That's it!"

"Tony, I might've believed you if two of my lieutenants, one in Atlanta and another in Miami hadn't told me that one of our top connects said you were trying to set up a meeting with him to do business directly with you."

"That's a lie! They lying to you, Genesis!"

"So two of my workers who operate in different states and don't fuck wit' each other are both telling me the same story but they're lying and you're telling me the truth."

"Yes. I am. They jealous man because I'm always making big moves for you so they tryna shut me down. I would never cross you."

"So the connect is lying, both our lieutenants and you can't give us any information about this so called nigga Dale we're supposed to be doing business with. This nigga on some bullshit, Genesis, point blank."

"Nico, I always been a good worker to you, why you tryna turn on me!"

"I ain't gonna even respond to you. Genesis, we not getting nothing out this knucklehead. He gon' still keep playing like we some dummies and honestly I'm fed up with the shit." There was silence for what seemed like forever so I edged closer, tilting my head around the corner wanting a visual to go with all the audio. My dad was standing directly in front of Tony. Nico was on his right hand side and Lorenzo was to his left. I could see a few of his security workers posted up against the wall with their weapons in hand.

"Tony, I gave you every opportunity to turn this fucked up situation around in your favor but Nico is right, you rather play us like we some dummies. I have too many things on the agenda to entertain this shit any longer."

"But, Genesis, I..." before Tony had a chance to finish his sentence all I saw was steel and my dad pulling the trigger. He riddled Tony's chained up body with bullets. I had to close my eyes and then open them back up to make sure I was seeing things correctly.

"Genesis, you did the right thing. That nigga wasn't gonna tell us shit about this so called Dale motherfucker. We just have to find another way to lure that nigga out of hiding."

"And we will." While my dad, Nico and Lorenzo continued to have a casual conversation with a blood drenched body slumped over in front of them, I was on my knees with my head down as my mind didn't believe what my eyes had just seen. Within those thirty seconds I understood why my dad didn't want me to be a part of his business—he was a murderer. I was well aware that part of the business he operated with Nico contained illegal activity but never murder. What really shocked me was that my dad blasted holes through Tony without flinching. That meant this wasn't his first killing and I wondered how many bodies he had under his belt because from where I stood he appeared to be a pro.

What I saw had me so completely shaken, I had

to get the hell out of there. I kept my composure leaving the warehouse as quietly as I came. When I got back to my car I had to sit there for a few minutes getting my mind right. *My dad is a murderer. I witnessed him kill another man without hesitation. Is this the sort of family business that I want to be a part of? Am I even ready for it and if not will I ever be?* Those were only a couple of the questions I thought about as I started the ignition and headed home. In the midst of my confusion I thought about one person and decided to call her.

"Hello."

"Hey, Aaliyah."

"I'm surprised to hear from you."

"I know. I wanted to apologize for how I spoke to you earlier."

"It's okay. I know you must have been super busy to cut me off like that."

"It doesn't matter. I can always make time for you. You're my best friend and I love you."

"I love you too."

"I'll call you tomorrow. Goodnight."

"Goodnight, Amir."

Hearing Aaliyah's voice was exactly what I needed. I really wanted to tell her everything I had just witnessed but loyalty to my father came first. I would have to deal with my anxiety alone but knowing that I had her did make it easier for me to cope.

Aaliyah

I Run My World

"Excuse me, has my attorney arrived yet?" I asked, clutching the iron bars of my holding cell.

"Nope." The officer stated without even looking at me as he walked by. I slumped down on the hard floor and put my head down.

"Can you please turn the air conditioner on? I'm burning up!" I screamed out as if anybody cared. My head was spinning and being boxed in a small hot ass coffin wasn't making it any better. I used my hand to wipe away some of the sweat that was dripping down my chest. I grabbed a hand full of loose curls and twisted them in a tight bun on top of my head. I felt dirty and hot but that was the least of my worries. Shit was critical for me right now and the only thing that was going to save me was a beast of an attorney who I thought would've been here by now.

I know my mother is pissed at me but would she really leave me in jail? No, she would never. But she has been tired of my shit for a while now. But has it gotten that bad that she would have me stuck behind these bars with no freedom in sight?

As I asked myself the question I couldn't help but think back to when I started rebelling against my parents especially my mother. I mean I was always opinionated, sassy and spoke my mind but I pretty much followed my parent's rules. But it was like one day a light switch turned on in my head and I decided I was going to do me whether I had my parent's blessings or not.

"Justina, are you ready yet?"

"I need another 30 minutes."

"For what and why the hell are you whispering?"

"Because my mother hasn't left yet. Hold on a sec that's her knocking at my door." There was a few minutes of silence and then I heard Justina's mother's voice.

"Why was your door locked?"

"It was to keep Justin out but I keep forgetting he isn't here."

"Oh, well I'm about to go. You'll probably be sleep by the time I get back so I'll see you in the morning."

"Ok, have fun tonight, mom. You look really pretty."

"Thanks, honey. And you could look really pretty too if you would take off those glasses and do something with your hair." I rolled my eyes when I heard Chantal say that bullshit to Justina. It was true but damn she could've found a more subtle way to say that to her own daughter. But from as far back as I could remember Chantal never conducted herself in a subtle way. She was always super extra and that's why my mother didn't fuck with her too tough.

"Hey, I'm back. I'm sure you heard. My mother is leaving so you can come get me whenever you're ready."

"Justina, I don't know why you just didn't tell your mother we're going out. All that sneaking isn't exactly cool. I mean we are seventeen."

"True but you don't understand my mother. If I told her we were meeting boys she would want to know what I was wearing. Then she would critique everything I put on and compare herself to me. I would then have to hear how hot she was when she was my age and that I basically can't compete. I don't feel like putting myself through the drama. I rather her think I'm asleep in the bed while she's hitting the town with her friends like she's still sixteen."

"I understand but I still think you need to start being honest with your mom."

"Aaliyah, my mother isn't cool like your mom. The only thing they have in common, is that my mom likes for you to call her by her first name and so does your mom when it comes to me but that is where the similarities end. You're lucky to have such great parents. Me on the other hand ..." Justina's voice trailed off and I decided to get off the subject.

"I'm on the way. See you in a little bit," and hung up the phone. I knew that Justina thought my life was so great and in comparison to hers maybe it was somewhat. I mean my mother wasn't a stuck up bitch like Chantal but my life had hardly been the fairytale that many thought it was for some time now. My dad seemed to travel more and more and I knew it was because when he was home all he and my mom would do was argue. It was to the point that I preferred him to be gone too just to get some peace. The person I felt most sorry for was my little brother. I grew up always having my dad around, I actually had two. I probably grew up getting too much attention and I could tell that Xavier wasn't getting enough. It pissed me off and made me become resentful towards my mother. I felt like she should've been trying harder to make it work with my dad but it seemed most of the time she was just going through the motions.

"Where are you going?" were the first words out of my mother's mouth when she saw me make a pit stop in the kitchen on my way to the garage.

"Justina and I are going out to dinner and a movie."

"Just the two of you?"

"We might meet up with some guy friends but I'm not sure yet."

"Have I ever met any of these guy friends?"

"Besides Amir, have you ever been interested in meeting any of my guy friends?"

"Amir doesn't count as a guy friend. You practically grew up with him, he's like family. And that's not what I asked you."

"No you haven't met them, are you satisfied."

"What I'm not satisfied with is your smart ass mouth. Ever since your dad bought you that car for your birthday you act like you can do whatever the hell you like without explaining yourself. But please don't forget that the same way you got them keys they can easily be snatched away."

"You're right, I'm sorry, mom," I said quickly changing my attitude. "I didn't mean to speak to you that way. It came off wrong. It's that time of the month," I lied. "These cramps have put me in a bad mood."

"I understand but next time, think before you speak."

"I will," I smiled. All I wanted to do was get out the house and if I had to fake a smile and give a bullshit apology to make it happen then that's what I would do.

When I got in the car I blasted my music and instantly forgot about the conversation I just had with my mother. My mind had switched to the cutie I had a date with tonight and how I was looking forward to it. His cousin was in town visiting and he wanted somebody he could chill with too, so that's why I was bringing Justina. When I got to her house and she opened the door she wasn't looking like nobody's special invited guest.

"Hey Aaliyah, you look great tonight!"

"So do you."

"You think...thanks!" I felt sorta bad telling such an obvious lie but what was I supposed to say? Your mother is right about you, you are the complete opposite of hot. I couldn't further shatter Justina's self-esteem and say that but I also knew it was time to whip my best friend in shape.

"We have a little time to waste, let's go upstairs and hang out in your bedroom for a minute."

"But I thought you said we were running late and

the guys were waiting for us."

"D'Mario called and said that something came up. So we're good." At the same time I was telling Justina that white lie I was sending D'Mario a text giving him some bullshit excuse as to why we were going to be late. It was for a good cause so I didn't care.

"Justina, I don't think I'm feeling what I have on, can I look at what you got in your closet?"

"I don't think I have anything in there that looks better than what you have on but you're more than welcome to look." Justina gave the response I figured she would and that's all I needed to do, what I had to do. When I stepped into her walk-in closet she had things in two sections. I called one the Justina section, which consisted of nothing but boring, plain clothes she wore on a regular. On the other side there were clothes I had never seen her in before. Most still had the tags on them. I decided this must be the Chantal section.

"Girl, I ain't never seen you in none of these clothes."

"I know. My mom picked that stuff out for me. Why I don't' know since I would never wear any of it."

"And why not?" I asked as I studied outfit after outfit of nothing but official hot shit.

"It's not my style." *Well it need to be*, I thought to myself.

"I have an idea, Justina."

"What?"

"Why don't we play dress up?"

"Excuse me?"

"Yeah. I'm going to put together an outfit for you,

do your hair, add a little makeup, it'll be fun!"

"What's wrong with what I have on now? You said I looked great."

"And you do. I just want to try something different. Plus you know I want to get into fashion, you can be my first test model."

"I'm not model material, Aaliyah."

"Come on, Justina, would you just cooperate. We need something to do until D'Mario and his cousin is ready for us anyway."

"I guess," Justina agreed reluctantly. I didn't give a damn that Justina was a reluctant participant. All I wanted to do was have an opportunity to work some magic. When I sat Justina down in front of me, the first thing I did was take off her glasses. "Can you put those back on? You know I can hardly see without them."

"Listen, I got this, plus you have a pair of contacts anyway. I don't know why you don't wear them."

"Why wear contacts when these glasses work just fine."

"Because these glasses hide your beautiful face and more people need to see it."

"You think I'm beautiful?" Justina stared at me with this stunned expression.

"Of course I think you're beautiful. Look at yourself." I turned Justina around so she was facing the mirror. I know she had seen her own reflection a million times but clearly she didn't appreciate what she saw staring back at her.

"I don't see beautiful. My mother is beautiful. You're beautiful but me I'm so regular."

"There is nothing regular about you but your attitude. If you don't know how beautiful you are then how is anybody else. Just sit there and let me handle this. Deal?"

"Deal."

For 45 minutes I worked on Justina as if she was competing to be crowned the Next Top Model. I unraveled the French braid that she always had going down the center of her head. Justina inherited the same honey blond highlights as her mother but you couldn't tell because the tight braid kept them hidden. I decided to give her a swooped bang and have the remaining hair loosely tousled up on the top with a few Bobbie pins holding it in place. I dabbed on some mascara to open up her wide eyes even more and added a little blush to accentuate her already bronzed skin. Once I put some gloss on her naturally pink lips her entire face glowed.

"Here put this on, but don't look at yourself yet." When I handed Justina the lime green silk romper her face frowned up but she stuck to our deal and put it on. As she zipped it up the fabric began hugging curves that were a well-kept secret underneath ill-fitting clothes. With a pair of strappy heels and some gold accessories Justina had been transformed into a true stunner.

"Wow!" Was all Justina continued to say for the next few minutes while examining herself.

"Say what you want about your mother, but she has some damn good taste. That romper and these shoes are ridic."

"My mother would have a freakin' heart attack if she caught a glimpse of me."

"I'm almost tempted to track her ass down so she can. You truly look amazing. You have to keep this up."

"But how?"

"If I have to come over every day and get you dressed then that's what I'll do."

"Aaliyah, you're so silly."

"I'm so serious! You have to stop letting all this go to waste," I said waving my hand up and down the length of Justina's body as if I was one of the Price Is Right spokes model showcasing a prize.

"I love my new look! I'ma make every effort to keep it up."

"Good and it's not that hard. All I did was put on a little blush, mascara and lip gloss. The hair was the hardest part but you need to start going with me when I hit the beauty salon. I go like once a week. And you have more than enough clothes and shoes to put together some killer outfits. You'll be shittin' on every girl at our school."

"Aaliyah, you're the best friend ever. Thank you." Justina gave me the biggest hug which put a huge smile on my face. It felt so good to see her so happy. I always knew that there was this gorgeous girl waiting to step out of her shell and I was thrilled to be the one to make it happen.

By the time we got to D' Mario and his cousin they had been waiting for over an hour. But I knew it would be all love once they both saw how on point Justina and I were looking. When we pulled up they were standing in front of D'Mario's midnight black Range Rover. I drove up and rolled down my window, greeting them both with a smile.

"Ma, this you?" D'Mario asked as he drooled over my pristine white Lamborghini."

"Don't the tags say Aaliyah," I stated. When D'Mario stepped to me I was on my way into the mall so he never had a chance to see what type of whip I was pushing. On our numerous phone conversations I never felt the need to tell him. I knew eventually he would see for himself.

"Damn, who the fuck is yo' peoples? You making me feel like a broke nigga next to yo' shit."

"It's all good boo. This ain't no competition especially since it ain't one you can win anyway." I winked my eye and gave him a sweet smile so although I dissed him he wasn't feeling mad just disappointed that a fly bitch was taking his shine. But I knew the tongue play I planned on blessing him with later on tonight would erase that.

When Justina and I stepped out my ride I could tell by the gleam in their eyes they didn't know what looked better, us or the car. I felt it was a tossup. I glanced over at Justina feeling so proud of what I had accomplished. I mean she had a lot to work with but to see what I envisioned walking right next to me, killing the game made me pleased.

"What's up, you looking more beautiful than I remember," D'Mario said giving me a hug. I gave him a hug back and already knew things were working in his favor because he smelled good. I loved a dude that kept a great scent. It was like that shit hypnotized me.

"Thank you. This is my best friend, Justina."

"What's up, Justina? This here is my cousin Ja Khel." Ja Khel and Justina shook hands and I could tell my girl was feeling uneasy. I figured it was because Justina wasn't used to guys lusting after her yet. But if she maintained her new appearance it would soon become the norm. Justina had gone all these years being the cute plain girl that nobody really paid attention to, to in less than an hour being a chick that any straight dude with a dick would catch a hard on for.

"So you young ladies ready to eat 'cause I'm starved, especially since you had us waiting all night," D'Mario grinned. I grabbed his hand and playfully blew him a kiss. I could see Justina and Ja Khel making small talk behind us but I hoped they would eventually click. Ja Khel was easy on the eyes so I was optimistic.

"This a five star spot, I like this," I said when we entered the restaurant.

"I know this is what an official chick like you is used to. So I'm only keeping it inline.

When the hostess sat us down, from our table we had a view of the garden with a waterfall that flowed into a makeshift river. It was beautiful. It made you feel as if you were in Italy. This was the type of spot that made you want to have some champagne or wine with your dinner but because I was only seventeen that was out the question. I was almost tempted to ask D'Mario to order some so I could get a sip of his but I quickly remembered he was only eighteen.

"So what are you ladies ordering tonight?"

"I'm not sure, what about you, Justina."

"Everything sounds so good."

"I know right," I laughed scrolling through the menu. Right when I was about to announce my selection I looked up to a pair of eyes staring me in my face. "Grandfather, what are you doing here?" I asked, getting up from my chair to give him a hug. No matter how often I saw my grandfather he always put a huge smile on my face. He was the one that had actually gotten the Lamborghini for my birthday. My grandfather wasn't even aware that I knew it was a gift from him. He assumed that I thought it came from Nico just like my mom did.

"Having dinner, and you're about to do the same," he said as he discreetly eyed everyone. "Hello, Justina, I almost didn't recognize you." Justina blushed but my grandfather didn't notice because he was carefully checking out the two guys that were with us.

"Grandfather, this is D'Mario and his cousin Ja Khel. They're friends of mine." My grandfather nodded his head but didn't speak to them. That didn't surprise me as he wasn't the most social person especially with people he didn't know.

"I'm not going to interrupt any longer. You enjoy your dinner."

"You never interrupt. You're more than welcome to join us. I always enjoy your company."

"Thank you, princess," he said kissing me on my forehead, "Next time." Then he walked away. I tried to see who he was having dinner with but he was sitting on the other side of the restaurant and I didn't want to come off as being completely nosey.

"So that's your grandfather, he seems like a cool cat." D'Mario commented.

"Yeah, he is. I'm a lucky girl. I have the best grandfather ever."

"She really does. He's the one that bought her that hot car she's driving."

"Justina, I told you that was our secret."

"Sorry, I forgot."

"Yeah, just don't forget when you're around my mother."

"So your mother doesn't know that your grandfather bought you a car that cost that much money. So who does she think you got it from?"

"My dad, but it's a long story. I'll tell you another time."

"Damn, all your people seem to be banking. Must be nice."

"It is. Here's our waitress, let's order," I suggested, ready to move on from the obvious.

After we finished our meal and while we were waiting for desserts, Justina and I headed to the ladies room. I did have to go but I also wanted to know if Justina was feeling Ja Khel. I was having a hard time reading her body language. I could mos def tell that Ja Khel was checking for her but I needed to know if the feeling was mutual.

"I'm really glad you brought me tonight. I'm having such a good time," Justina said when we were halfway to the bathroom.

"That's what's up, so does that mean you like Ja Khel?"

"I mean he's definitely cute but I'm not sure he's my type."

"What do you mean?"

"He might be a little too fast for me."

"Why you say that? Hold up, let me use the bathroom first then you can explain."

"I gotta go too so cool."

Justina and I came out the bathroom stall at the same time. Between washing our hands and touching up our face and hair in the mirror Justina began telling me why Ja Khel had the potential to be a no go for her.

"Well, when he was asking me about myself and what I liked to do I started opening up a little. I felt comfortable so I asked him was he in school and he said no."

"And..."

"I mean don't you think it's weird that he like eighteen and not in any type of school?"

"He might've already graduated high school and decided not to go to college but get a job instead."

"I thought about that so I asked him what he did." There was this long pause and I started tapping my nails on the counter top. Justina was too busy making goo-goo eyes at herself in the mirror that she must've forgot what the hell she was about to say and didn't notice I was growing impatient waiting for her to continue.

"Any day now!"

"Oh, girl, my fault. So when I asked him what he did he was like he worked in the family business. I was like what sort of family business and he said the sort that required him to travel a lot."

"So from that you got the impression he might be too fast for you?"

"Yeah, because if you're traveling all the time then that means you're probably meeting a ton of different girls and not wanting to take any of them seriously."

"Chile please, you can meet a bunch of different girls right her in the state of California. You don't have to be on the road to do that."

"True, but it sure gives you plenty of opportunity to do so. Listen, he just seems like a player to me. I don't need a man like that. My father was a player and I see how neurotic it has made my mother. I don't want a guy like that."

"To be fair, I think your mother has done her fair share of playing too." Justina gave me a nasty glare.

"Maybe so but it's not only that. I'm actually interested in somebody else, who I like a lot," she stressed. "And when he sees my new makeover I think he'll definitely be convinced I'm the one."

"Who, do I know him?" But before she could answer me, in walked my worst nightmare.

"If it isn't my beautiful niece Aaliyah. You're looking more and more like Precious and Supreme... oops I meant Nico each time I see you."

"Maya, why are you stalking me? What are you doing here?" Right before she responded the answer popped in my head.

"I'm having dinner with my father. I guess he didn't tell you that when he stopped by your table."

"Of course he didn't tell me. He didn't want to ruin my meal. Come on Justina, let's go. This bathroom suddenly has a very bad odor to it."

"Little girl, you need to learn respect."

"Now why would I respect a psychotic criminal like you?"

"You know I beat those charges many, many years ago. So I'm no more of a criminal than you are."

"You beat those charges because of my grandfather's money. You bamboozled him with your lies but luckily my mother sees right through you and so do I."

"All I ever wanted was a relationship with my sister and there was a time I hoped to have a relationship with you but I was never given the chance."

"After all this time you still love playing the victim role. My mother should've done us all a favor and got rid of you when she had a chance. Now excuse me."

"Be careful little girl, it can be dangerous out there."

"You can stop with the little girl BS. You have a pair of good eyes, and you can clearly see I'm not a little girl. And before you make subliminal threats, remember one thing, you're not my sister. I feel no sort of obligation towards you so I advise *you* to be careful."

"Wow, that was intense," Justina finally said after not breathing a word while we were in the bathroom.

"Fuck Maya! I'll never understand how my grandfather deals with her. It's so obvious what a sick bitch she is."

"I know. When you told me all the things she's put your family through I don't get it either. But she is his daughter. I can't imagine my dad ever turning his back on me no matter what I did."

"Yeah, but you're not some psycho lunatic," I huffed walking up to our table.

"We were getting concerned. I was about to have the waitress go to the bathroom and check on you," D'Mario remarked when we sat back down at the table.

"I ran into somebody I knew and we were catching up."

"Oh, so you ready for dessert."

"No, actually I want the check I'm ready to go."

"The movie doesn't start for another hour."

"I don't care. I can't stay in this restaurant for another second. As a matter of fact, I'll meet you outside. I grabbed my purse and I could see Justina following behind me. Maya seemed to suck all the air out of me and I needed to go outside to get it back. That woman had singlehandedly divided my family. What she did so many years ago was still causing my parent's marriage to deteriorate right before my eyes. I hated Maya for what she did to my mother and I prayed one day she would pay for it with her life.

I woke up with Maya's face consuming my mind. It was like every couple of years she would pop up to antagonize me but it seemed that her spirit lingered around me every day. If Maya made me feel this way I could only imagine the affect she had on my mother. While brushing my teeth and combing my hair before going downstairs I thought about the numerous times

I heard Maya's name mentioned in our household. The stories of mayhem she caused and how in the past it haunted me but as I got older instead it left me infuriated.

As I made my way downstairs to the kitchen, my mind must have been very deep in Maya land because I was shocked when I walked in on an intense conversation between my mother and grandfather.

"Good morning!" I said in a super chipper voice so neither could detect that for some reason I felt their conversation was about me and it made me nervous.

"It is a good morning now that I've seen my lovely granddaughter."

"You just saw me last night," I laughed affectionately.

"I can never see my granddaughter enough."

"So is that why you're over here this morning, 'cause you wanted to see me again?"

"You know damn well that's not why he is here."

"Calm down, Precious." My mother cut her eyes at my grandfather.

"Don't tell me to calm down! Aaliyah is my daughter and she had no business out with those men."

"What are you talking about? I only had dinner with some friends."

"If this dinner was so innocent why didn't you tell me that's where you were going before you left here last night?"

"It was a last minute decision. At first I was only going out with Justina but D'Mario called me when I was on my way to pick her up and invited us to dinner. It was no big deal."

"You're so full of it, Aaliyah! Nothing with you is

no big deal."

"What is your deal? All we did was have dinner. Grandfather," I said turning my attention in his direction. "Is this what you came over for? To get my mother worked up because I went out to dinner with some guys."

"No. I'm here to protect you."

"Protect me. From what, a date?"

"Do you know how old those men are?" My mother asked right when I could tell my grandfather was about to speak.

"Eighteen."

"More like twenty-two."

"No they're not."

"Yes they are! Your grandfather told me!"

"How would grandfather know?" My mother turned towards my grandfather waiting for him to speak up.

"I know who both of those men are and I can tell you as fact, that they haven't seen eighteen in a few years."

"I'm assuming since they lied about their ages they also didn't tell you that they're drug dealers," my mother jumped in. I felt like I was being tagged team with a bunch of bullshit I knew absolutely nothing about. "Aaliyah, answer me!"

"Of course I didn't know. I met him at the mall. I thought he had just graduated from high school. D'Mario being a drug dealer was the furthest thing from my mind."

"So where did you think he got that Range Rover

he was driving in?"

"I drive a Lamborghini, what's your point. This is Beverly Hills. It's not abnormal to see a young guy driving an expensive car." It wasn't until I saw the fire burning in my mother's eyes that I remembered who I was talking to. "It was an honest mistake, mom. I apologize." I lowered the tone of my voice trying to do damage control but my mother wasn't having it.

"You can give me the keys to your car because you won't be driving it anytime soon. Is that the point you needed if not I just gave it to you."

"You can't take away my car!"

"I can and I will."

"Everybody relax," my grandfather said reaching over the breakfast bar to take our hands. I took his hand but my mother ignored his gesture.

"I'm perfectly relaxed, Quentin, but I'm not going to let my daughter disrespect me."

"Mommy, I'm sorry. I didn't mean to disrespect you."

"Oh, so now I'm mommy. You should've remembered that when you were running off at the mouth a minute ago."

"I told you I was sorry. I mean I had a lot on my mind. Seeing Maya yesterday put me in a really bad mood." I glanced over at my grandfather and I hated to throw him under the bus. But I couldn't take being without my car and that was the only thing I could think to say to garner some sympathy from my mother.

"Where did you see Maya?"

"At the restaurant where I saw grandfather, she

came into the bathroom. We exchanged words and it's left me really shaken. That's why I snapped at you because the Maya thing has me in a really bad way." What I said wasn't a complete lie but it wasn't all true either.

"I'm assuming Maya was at the restaurant with you," my mother said now turning her burning eyes at my grandfather.

"Yes, but I had no idea she had an encounter with Aaliyah. Maya didn't even mention she saw her."

"I wonder why." My mother stated sarcastically. "You continue to keep that poison around you and then had her around my daughter. And you want to come to my house saying you're trying to protect Aaliyah by keeping her away from some dope boys but the person she really needs protection from is like your best fuckin' friend."

"She's not my best friend. She's my daughter, just like you are. And you know I would never let any harm come to Aaliyah."

"Then why couldn't you protect Aaliyah yesterday when Maya harassed her in the bathroom? Oh I forgot, Maya is misunderstood, she would never harass Aaliyah or anybody else for that matter. We're all crazy. She's the only sane one."

"Precious, please."

"Please my ass. You tell that daughter of yours to stay the hell away from Aaliyah. Now would you please get out of my house because I no longer want to have a conversation with you," my mother said before exiting the kitchen.

"Grandfather, I'm so sorry. I shouldn't have said anything."

"Don't be sorry, it's not your fault. I had no idea that you and Maya had words. But you have to know Maya would never hurt you or your mother."

"Grandfather, I love you, I really do. And I wish I wouldn't have brought Maya's name up because your relationship with mom is already so fragile I hate making it worse. But you're wrong about Maya. She does want to hurt us."

"I know your mother has a lot of bad history with Maya and she's shared most of it with you but that's in the past. Maya has made a lot of mistakes but she only wants to be a part of this family."

"That will never happen."

"Because your mother doesn't want to give her sister a chance and because of that you don't want to give Maya an opportunity to have a relationship with you which is understandable."

"You don't understand. When I looked in Maya's eyes last night I saw for myself how sick she is. I don't understand how you don't see it. I know she's your daughter but can your love for Maya blind you from the truth? I've always respected how wise you are but you're so wrong about Maya. She's trouble, grandfather."

"I hate you feel that way, my princess," grandfather said kissing me on my forehead. "But I promise you I won't let anybody hurt you or your mother and that includes Maya. I'll talk to you later and be nice to your mother. I love you."

"I will and I love you too." Seeing my grandfather's

sprit broken as he walked out made me feel terrible. He always appeared so in control but now he seemed powerless. And he was when it came to the Maya situation. No matter how hard he tried to be the link to put them together my mother wanted nothing to do with her sister and I didn't blame her one bit.

"Is Quentin gone?" I heard my mother ask as I was getting some orange juice out of the refrigerator.

"Yes, he just left."

"I can't believe he had Maya around you last night."

"Mom, it wasn't like grandfather knew I was going to be at the restaurant and that Maya would approach me in the bathroom."

"That's not the point. If he would've cut her off the only place she would be walking around is a jail cell. And to think I was so appreciative he came over here to warn me about those men you were out with last night. I'll never let myself have a real relationship with him as long as he is breaking bread with that psycho."

"Mother, I totally agree with you that Maya is a psycho. When I looked in her eyes last night, I swear I saw the devil. But grandfather loves you so much. Maybe you could still try and have a real daughter/ father relationship with him in spite of Maya. Maya probably feels like she's winning right now because she's hindering you all's relationship."

"I don't give a damn if Maya feels like she's winning. My concern is you and your safety because I know how to handle Maya."

"I know you do and so does Maya."

"Well if she needs a reminder I'll be more than

happy to give it to her. You and your brother mean everything to me. I won't let Maya hurt either one of you."

"What about dad?"

"Huh?"

"You said that Xavier and I mean everything to you but you didn't mention dad."

"Of course I love Supreme."

"Then why didn't you mention him?" my mother stayed silent as if she was at a loss for words which never happened. "I know you guys have been having problems for a long time."

"Aaliyah, what are you talking about?"

"I've heard the arguments. Just because I don't say anything doesn't mean I don't know what's happening."

"Your father and I have been married for years, disagreements happen. It's called marriage and it ain't always pretty. But we're good."

"Are you sure? Dad seems to be home less and less. Sometimes it feels like he doesn't live here anymore."

"Yes I'm sure. Your father and I have been through a lot but we always stay together and remain strong. Stop worrying, we're fine. First Maya, now your dad, you have too much on your mind. You should call Justina and go do some shopping. It's too beautiful outside for you to be in the house."

"Does that mean I can take my car?"

"That's right I did put you on punishment. But under the circumstances I'll give you a reprieve." My mother smiled and rubbed my cheek.

"You're the best!"

"But, Aaliyah, you do have to be careful. I understand the allure of dealing with hustlers but you don't have to do that. You don't want for anything so there is no need for you to chase that life. I promise you it doesn't lead to anything but problems."

"Now I'm going to give you the same advice you gave me. Stop worrying," I grinned. Honestly I didn't know they were drug dealers and now that I do I'll keep my distance."

"Good. Now go have some fun." I gave my mom a hug before running upstairs to my room. I wasn't sure if I was super happy because I was able to get out of my punishment before it started or because I had been given the green light to do some damage on the credit card. But I figured it was a combination of both. Right when I was about to call Justina up to let her know today's plan, I saw D'Mario's name popping across my screen. I was tempted to ignore it but his dimples and pretty smile kept flashing in my head.

"Hello."

"Hey beautiful, how are you this morning?"

"Good, what about you?"

"Amazing."

"Amazing. I don't think I've ever heard that response before but I like it."

"You should. I try to make every day amazing. So what are you getting into today?"

"About to get dressed then pick up Justina so we can do some Saturday afternoon shopping."

"Let me come with you."

"Only if you're doing the buying."

"Of course, I wouldn't have it any other way."

"You sure because I'm vicious when it comes to spending cash."

"I already know."

"Cool, but don't say I didn't warn you." When I got off the phone with D'Mario I immediately called Justina.

"What's up girl, I was just on the phone with Amir."

"What was he talking about?"

"Wanting to know when we were coming his way."

"It's almost that time of year again so soon."

"Yeah, that's what I told him. I can't wait for Amir to see my new look. He told me to take a pic with my phone and send it. As soon as I get myself dolled up I'm going to. He is going to have a fit."

"I'm sure he will. And some new outfits to go with your new look can't hurt either."

"But I have a ton of clothes in my closet I haven't even worn yet."

"True, but they were all picked out by your mother. Aren't you ready to pick out your own hot shit?"

"Yeah! That's exactly what I need to do."

"Glad you think so because I'll be over to scoop you up in an hour."

"Great. Let me go catch my mom before she leaves... can't go shopping without any money. See you soon." When I hung up with Justina I laid on my bed for a second before getting in the shower. I started thinking about my conversation with D'Mario. There was no reason for me to let him come with us shopping. It wasn't like I needed his money but I guess I just wanted to see if he would do it. I decided to call him back and dead it. I mean he was a drug dealer and I told my mom I would leave him alone, but he was so cute and sexy. I decided one more date wouldn't hurt anything and I tossed my phone down. *Yeah it was time I started living a little bit. I needed to stop worrying about my parent's problems and create some fun ones of my own.*

Amir

Proposition

"I need one more chance." I shook my head as I remembered Aaliyah saying those words to me last night. Now I would give anything to turn back time and have that conversation with her again. Things would've gone so differently and this hell we were now in wouldn't exist. But the conversation did happen and now here I was waiting in my car thinking back wishing I could see Aaliyah again.

"Open up," I heard Aaliyah yelling as she pounded on the door. As hard as her fist was banging I would've thought there was a 6'5" man trying to get in instead of a 5'5" girl.

"Chill the fuck out, Aa..." I immediately stopped myself when I opened the door. "I apologize, Mrs. Mills, I didn't realize you were with Aaliyah."

"Don't worry, Amir. I know my fair share of curse

words."

"Why didn't you tell me your mother was with you," I whispered in Aaliyah's ear as they came in. She just gave me a frown like leave her the fuck alone.

"So where's your dad? Oh never mind, here he is now. Genesis, hello."

"It's good to see you," my dad smiled giving Precious a hug. "This is my good friend Lorenzo. Lorenzo, this is Precious Mills and her daughter Aaliyah."

"It's a pleasure to meet you both."

"Thank you," both mother and daughter said in unison.

"Genesis, Aaliyah told me that you're taking them to the K97 Summer Jam concert. Is that true?" My dad gave me a peculiar stare and I put my head down. Now I understood why Aaliyah's mom came through, she was on parental control.

"Actually I'm not taking them but one of my trusted workers will escort them to the concert." Aaliyah and I gave each other a look of relief when my dad came through for us because I hadn't even discussed us going to the concert with him.

"I see. So they will be supervised?"

"Of course." I think my dad could tell Aaliyah's mom wasn't completely convinced so he switched the subject which I figured was an attempt to get her mind off that topic. "So, Precious, how long are you going to be in New York?"

"For a week or so."

"Did Supreme come with you?"

"No he actually took Xavier on vacation for a little

father/son time."

"That's good. I'm sure they're enjoying themselves."

"Yeah, I'm sure they are. I know Nico won't be back for a couple days so I brought Aaliyah early hoping we could have some mother/daughter time before she spent the rest of her break with Nico. But her calendar seems to already be filled up."

"Mom, I told you Amir already had the tickets and it wouldn't be fair to cancel on him at the last minute. You're the one who didn't believe me."

"You're right but Genesis has confirmed what you said so I apologize. You all go to the concert and have a good time. I'll see you at home later on tonight. Goodnight everybody."

"Precious," my dad called out as I was walking her to the door. "If you're not doing anything, why don't you have dinner with Lorenzo and Me? He just got back in town and I was going to take him to my favorite spot for dinner. I have to wrap up some business first but it won't take that long."

"That's ok, I don't want to intrude."

"Trust me you're not intruding. We'll enjoy your company. Isn't that right Lorenzo?" Lorenzo simply nodded his head.

"Ok. Dinner at a nice restaurant with two handsome men might be what I need," she laughed.

"I think so too, mom. Maybe then you'll lighten up on me a little."

"Never that."

"So, Aaliyah, you just about ready to head out?"

"Sure, but let me use your bathroom for a second."

"Precious, you can go have a seat in the living room. It won't take me long to finish up what I have to do. Can I get you something to drink?"

"No, I'm good. Let me know when you're ready."

"I will," my dad said before turning to me. "Amir, can I see you in my office for a minute." I followed behind my dad already knowing what he was about to say. "Close the door."

"Dad, listen…"

"No, you listen. Don't put me in the middle of something without discussing it with me first."

"I had no idea Mrs. Mills was going to show up. Aaliyah didn't even warn me."

"That's not the point. You should've told me you planned on going to the concert with Aaliyah. That is the truth isn't it?"

"Of course, we just didn't think we were going to have a chaperone."

"Well now you are. I'll have Dice take you."

"That's not necessary. You always let me go places by myself or with my friends.'"

"I told Precious that you will be supervised and that's that. Understand something, Amir. Aaliyah is the daughter of my business partner and close friend. I'm also fond of her mother so I don't want any problems. What I might let you do can't always apply when others are involved. Are you following me?"

"Yes. So can I ask you a question?"

"Of course."

"Why did you invite Precious to dinner? I mean Lorenzo strikes me as the type of man that is all about business who wouldn't want that to be put aside because you felt the need to invite your son's best friend's mother to join you."

"I always make sure business is in order so Lorenzo will be fine."

"That's cool but you still didn't tell me why you invited Precious."

"Because although Precious is a strong woman and she appears to have everything together she's vulnerable and needs a friend right now."

"How can you tell?'

"Because I've been there before."

"Like after my mother died?"

"That was no doubt the lowest point in my life. If it wasn't for you I wouldn't have gotten through it. But enough heavy talk. You and Aaliyah go have a good time at the concert." My dad didn't know how bad I wanted to have a 'heavy talk' with him. My mind still hadn't completely grasped that I witnessed him commit murder. I had no one I could talk to about it so I desperately wanted to share what I saw with him. But to do that I would expose the fact that I listened in on his business meeting and then followed him to the warehouse. I knew my dad would be heated that I had basically spied on him. The only option I had was to keep my mouth shut at least for now. Besides, this wasn't even the right time. Bringing up my mother had put him in a somber mood.

"Ok, dad, talk to you later." I left my dad's office regretting that I mentioned my mother. It never failed, every time I brought her name up, the life seemed to drain from his face. Nothing hurt more than seeing my father, a man to me that represented the epitome of power and strength become weak right before my eyes.

"Ok girl, we'll see you soon. I'll tell you how it was tomorrow."

"Who was that?" I asked Aaliyah when I came out my dad's office and heard her on the phone.

"Justina, she'll be here tomorrow."

"Cool."

"She's mad disappointed that she's missing the concert tonight but I told her they'll be a ton of fun things we'll do when she gets in town."

"For sure."

"You sound real enthusiastic...not."

"Sorry, I just have some things on my mind."

"Things like what?"

"I don't want to talk about it right now. Let's just go have a good time."

"Okay but you know I'm always here for you."

"I know big head," I laughed putting Aaliyah in a playful head lock.

"Joke if you want, Amir, but you've been acting mad different for the past few weeks. Something is up with you and I wish you would tell me what it is."

"Maybe later. But we need to go. As usual we're already running late."

"We'll be fine. I ain't that pressed anyway. It's not like it's a Sway Stone concert which is coming up in a few months. That sure would be a great eighteenth birthday present...hint, hint."

"Your birthday is in two weeks and Sway's concert

here isn't for several months."

"I know but I still want to go. It can be a late birthday present. I'll still be celebrating anyway."

"I'm sure you will. Now let's go."

"That concert was so good! It's like the performers always bring their best game to that show."

"Yeah, that's because they know New Yorkers will blast they ass. They ain't got no choice but to come correct."

"Amir, you ain't neva lied. It's like they be looking for a reason to start booing. So what you wanna do now, 'cause I ain't ready to call it a night, are you?"

"No. I wish my dad would've let me drive. Then we could hit a couple of parties. But I'm not trying to be chaperoned by one of my dad's workers anywhere."

"I feel you. Wait, I have an idea."

"What?"

"My dad is out of town. We can get in the hot tub, listen to some music and chill out."

"Now that sounds like a good idea," I said before we got in the car.

"Where would you like me to take you now, Amir?" Dice asked being the perfect driver.

"To Aaliyah's house. Her mom is going to meet us there."

"Are you sure, I can take you back to your father's place."

"I'm positive."

"Yes, Dice he's sure. There are some things I want to do for my dad before he gets home. He loves surprises."

"Then to Mr. Carter's house we go."

"Once we get to my dad's place, I'll text my mom and let her know we're there," Aaliyah whispered to me.

"Cool, I'll do the same with my dad."

During the ride to Alpine I remained pretty quiet. It felt good to be in the moment and enjoying time with Aaliyah.

"Hey, we're here," I heard Aaliyah say. I was in such a mellow place that I didn't even realize we made it. "Dice roll down the window so I can put the code in."

A few seconds later the gate opened and Dice drove along the curved driveway before pulling up in front of the mansion. "Amir, would you like for me to wait here for you?"

"No you can go 'head, Dice. I'll get back home."

"Are you sure? I have no problem waiting."

"Positive, I'll work it out."

"Ok, but call me if you need me."

"Will do," I said shutting the door.

"I can always take you home. You know my dad keeps a car here for me to drive."

"Yeah, like I said we'll work it out. I was just ready to get rid of Dice. He's good people but having him up under me like this makes me feel like I'm twelve again."

"That's how my mom is making me feel. She wants to keep me under her thumb and I'm like relax. That's why I was happy when your dad invited her to have dinner with him and his friend, who is fine by the way. What was his name again?"

"Lorenzo."

"Yeah, that dude looks good. I've never seen him before. How long has he been friends with your dad?"

"I think for a while. But he only recently came back on the scene. So dudes like Lorenzo is what you like?" I tried to ask the question without sounding as if I really cared but I wasn't sure if it came off that way.

"I prefer my men a little older and Lorenzo is sexy but he's a little too much older for me."

"I see. Could you imagine the fit both your dad's would have if you started dating a man Lorenzo's age?"

"Forget them, shit my mother would be the one I would need to hide from," Aaliyah laughed. "Speaking of my mother, let me call her before she tries to put out an Amber Alert on me."

"Yeah, let me call my dad too," I said taking my phone out my pocket. When I called my dad it went straight to voicemail so I left him a message. I found it strange my dad's phone went straight to voicemail as he made it a point to keep it charged for business purposes. "Did you talk to your mom?" I asked Aaliyah wanting to know if she was able to make contact since I wasn't.

"No, it went straight to voicemail so I left her a message."

"That happened with my dad too. I guess that's a good thing. Maybe they're having so much fun that they won't bother us."

"Yeah, that would be nice but I think my mother has forgotten what the definition of fun is so that's highly doubtful. She probably has it on vibrate and didn't realize I was calling. Trust me she'll be blowing me up in a few minutes."

"Then I guess we better start having some fun asap." As we made our way to the back I looked up at the multiple levels with artistic murals adorning the walls. No matter how many times I came to Nico's house I never grew tired of admiring them. It gave you the vibe like you were visiting a mansion in Rome or something.

"You know where the swim trunks are," Aaliyah commented when we walked past the swimming pool with flowing fountains towards the Jacuzzi.

"Of course." There were two pool houses in the back, one for men and the other for women. The shit was so sick, it was crazy. Each had a ton of swimming trunks and bathing suits that people could borrow if they forgot to bring their own. When Aaliyah came out in her light pink bikini she reminded me of cotton candy. I didn't want to get turned on by her but I couldn't help myself. Her skin looked like caramel and it didn't help that her breast and ass were popping out just right.

"What are you staring at?" she questioned.

"Oh, I didn't know you had a diamond earring in your belly button," I replied trying to play off the fact that I was foaming at the mouth over her body. But that was a mild distraction compared to all the curves that had my third leg feeling some type of way.

"Oh, I forgot to tell you. I got it a few weeks ago as an early birthday present to myself. My mom doesn't even know yet. She's going to flip the fuck out when she finds out. I figure I'd tell her on my eighteenth birthday. I mean at that point what can she really do."

"I feel you," I said getting into the Jacuzzi. "Damn, this water feels good. It's not too hot, just right."

"I can't wait to get in."

"What you waiting for?"

"I'm about to get this bottle of champagne so we can have an early birthday toast."

"Make sure you get the good shit."

"Excuse me, that's all my daddy got! He don't even fuck around with the mid-level shit. You know how he do. It's first class all the way.

When Aaliyah got in the Jacuzzi and handed me my glass for the first time I was looking at her as not being my best friend but a girl that I wanted to get with. It was fucking my head up a little because we were supposed to be like brother and sister. But my body was telling me something different.

"Let's make a toast."

"Okay."

"I feel like maybe we should wait until Justina gets here tomorrow. Nah, we can do one now and do another one when she comes."

"Works for me."

"Cool, so like I was saying," Aaliyah smiled. "Let's make a toast that eighteen will be the best year of our lives."

"Cheers," we both said as our glasses clinked together.

"This some good champagne right here," I said guzzling it down like it was water.

"I told you," here have some more," Aaliyah offered, filling my glass back up. "Can you believe I'm about to be eighteen and in a couple months you will be too. It seems like yesterday we were celebrating my eighth birthday. Now look at us ten years later."

"I know. Remember after the party was over we decided to keep it going."

"Oh gosh, how can I forget!"

"You and Justina thought it would be a great idea to play doctor and let me be your patient. Precious walked in on us and I was lying across your bed with only my underwear on."

"And in two seconds those were about to come off. My mom was livid."

"Livid is an understatement. She took away all your birthday presents."

"And I was pissed because my grandfather had gotten me this special collector's edition Barbie doll that I had been begging for. It took weeks for my dad to convince her to give it back to me."

"Wow, those were the good days."

"I think these days are still pretty good and this one might only get better."

"How's that?"

"I think we should play doctor again except for this time I'll be the patient."

"I don't know if that's a good idea."

"Why not? It's not like I'm eight anymore." Before I could answer, Aaliyah's lips were touching mine. Then my tongue somehow ended up down her throat and my hand was easing down the crack of her ass. It all felt so right and wrong at the same time."

"Aaliyah, we shouldn't be doing this," I managed

to say between sensuous kisses.

"Yes we should." I pulled away so I could read the words her eyes were speaking to me. "I've known you it seems like my entire life and I think it would only be right that I lost my virginity to you, tonight."

"Aaliyah, you're a virgin?"

"Yes. Why do you say that like it's so hard to believe?"

"You always seemed so advanced, you know mature. I figured you lost your virginity a long time ago."

"Nope! But you're right I am advanced and mature. I just didn't think anybody was worthy enough to have me, that is besides you."

"But I thought you told me you were seeing somebody."

"I am. Listen, I'm not a saint and I have messed around. You know heavy foreplay but I've never taken it *all* the way. But I want to tonight with you."

"Aaliyah, I'm flattered I really am."

"I'm not interested in you being flattered. I want you to tell me that you're checking for me the same way I'm checking for you."

"I can't do that."

"Excuse me!"

"You're gorgeous, there's no denying that. And I know you have a ton of guys checking for you but I'm seeing Justina."

"What!" Aaliyah screamed that out so loud I knew she had to wake up the whole neighborhood. "You're seeing Justina?" I nodded my head yes. "How long has that been going on and why didn't she tell me?"

"For a few months. We were going to tell you together when she got here."

"I can't believe this," Aaliyah said, picking up her glass and pouring herself some more champagne. I was tempted to re-up but was afraid I wouldn't be able to maintain self-control if I got anymore liquor in my system. It was already taking every ounce of strength I had in me not to oblige Aaliyah's request and take her virginity.

"I hope this doesn't change things between us. You truly are my best friend and I wouldn't want anything to mess that up."

"It makes sense now. When Justina told me she was interested in somebody I couldn't figure out who the hell she was talking about and I could tell she didn't want t me to know. Now I understand why. But can you just answer something for me?"

"Sure, what is it?"

"Why Justina and not me? I mean I love Justina, she's like a sister to me but we are so much more alike than the two of you."

"Yeah, we're too much alike."

"Huh?"

"Aaliyah, I don't want to date somebody like me. With you, I'll always be wondering if you're seeing somebody else or if you're lying to me. I know how much you scheme. I've been a witness to it."

"But I wouldn't do that with you."

"That's the thing. I'm not sure about that. And one thing my father always told me is you can't be with a woman who doesn't make you feel confident that she can be trusted."

"Oh, so now you're calling me untrustworthy?"

"All I'm saying is that I don't feel confident that I can trust you a hundred percent."

"But Justina makes you feel a hundred percent confident."

"Yes, she does."

"Why because she's timid and quiet?"

"Now you're being petty, Aaliyah."

"No, I'm being real. You've put Justina on this pedestal like she's some sort of saint and I'm walking around with a scarlet letter on my chest. It's not fair. No I'm not all meek like Justina but I'm no harlot either."

"I didn't say that."

"Maybe not in those exact words but that's exactly what you're alluding to. It's cool though."

"Aaliyah, don't do this," I said touching the side of her cheek. The way the moonlight hit her face it made it appear as if she was glowing. There was this strong urge for me to give into the lust I was feeling towards her but I knew it was wrong so I made myself resist.

"I wish you would've given us a chance. I know I could've made you happy."

"Maybe, but I'm with Justina so it doesn't matter."

"You're right and I have to respect that. Both of you mean so much to me and I'm not going to ruin our friendships because you chose her over me."

"Thank you. You really have matured, Aaliyah. Because not too long ago you couldn't even comprehend the word 'no' and not getting your way. I think you're right. Eighteen will be your best year yet."

I laid back in the Jacuzzi and closed my eyes. I was relieved that I let Aaliyah know the status of my relationship with Justina and I was proud that I didn't let my body overpower my mind. But it was crazy that I had two girls in my life and I had real love for both of them.

Aaliyah

When It All Comes Falling Down

The longer I sat in my jail cell the more hopeless my situation seemed to become. I started visualizing myself forever trapped in an orange jumpsuit with nothing but an inmate number to identify me. It was puzzling me how I went from magnificent to miserable in less than twenty four hours. I began recalling how only a few short months ago I had dodged a major blow but this time around it appeared I wouldn't be as fortunate.

"I'll be at your crib in about twenty minutes," I told D'Mario as I zipped up my jeans.

"You said that an hour ago."

"I know but I got held up. But I really am about to walk out the door. I'll see you in a few." I let out a sigh of relief and regret when I finally buttoned up my jeans because I knew damn well they were too fuckin' tight. My ass and hips seemed to be spreading rapidly and I figured it was because I had recently started taking the pill. I wasn't fucking just yet but I planned on to and I wanted to be prepared. Yeah, when the time was right, I would definitely make D'Mario strap up but I wanted back up protection too because getting pregnant was something I didn't even want to have to worry about.

As I put on my tank top and heels I rolled my eyes thinking that I wasn't even sure I wanted D'Mario to be the dude to take my virginity but I was slowly but surely leaning in that direction. Ever since Amir crushed my dreams of having him be my first I put all my focus on my relationship with D'Mario, which was extremely difficult since I had to sneak around. Although I was now eighteen and technically there wasn't anything illegal about our relationship, my mother had made it clear that she didn't want me dating a drug dealer. The funny thing was D'Mario still didn't know I knew the truth about what his job profession really was. I was too busy having fun with him to even bring it up. He was the only reason I was able to not be totally crushed by the news Amir and Justina were boyfriend and girlfriend. So I was savoring the good times to keep my mind off what I considered to be a very low point in my life.

Thirty minutes later, after pulling my look together I grabbed my purse and headed downstairs. As I was rushing to get out the door, I was thinking about how right D'Mario was that my twenty minutes were now about to turn into another hour. Time and I were not friends or even associates. I constantly fought against it like we were enemies. I made a decision right then; that would be something I would start working on—being on time.

"Aaliyah, where are you rushing off to?" I heard my dad ask me; right when I thought I had reached freedom.

"Hey, daddy, when did you get back?" I said turning around to give him a hug.

"Late last night. I didn't want to wake you."

"You should have. I missed you. It seems like you've been gone forever."

"Only a week."

"Yeah, but your week is like every other day. How much do you want to bet that you'll be going back out of town in a couple of days?"

"I'm not going to bet you, Aaliyah."

"Why? Because you know I would win."

"Why don't we go have lunch? We need some father/daughter time."

"That would be nice but I'm meeting Justina and I'm already running late."

"What about dinner."

"That would be cool. But let's make it a family dinner, you, me, mom and Xavier."

"We'll see."

"Why do we have to see, why can't we just make it happen?"

"Because Supreme has no interests in making it happen." I looked over my dad's shoulder and saw my mother standing in the distance.

"Precious, not now. I'm trying to have a pleasant conversation with my daughter. I don't want to argue with you."

"Is this what we're having, an argument? I thought it was called a family discussion."

"What is going on between the two of you? Is that why you're always going out of town, dad, because you can't stand to be in the house with mom?"

"Answer her, Supreme," my mom demanded, after my dad kept quiet for a few minutes.

"You want the truth, the answer is yes. Right now I rather be away working, then in the house with your mother." Even with the distance between us I could see a slight look of despair cross my mother's face.

"Daddy, what happened? You used to love mommy so much."

"I still love your mother. We're just going through a difficult time right now."

"Would you please stop talking about me like I'm not in the fuckin' room! That's what the problem is now. Instead of you talking to me you talk through me."

"What the hell are you talking about, Precious?"

"You know what I'm talking about. You speak to me like I'm invisible. Like what I feel and think doesn't even matter to you."

"That's all in your mind."

"I guess it's in my mind too that you haven't touched me in months not even on the rare occasions that you're actually sleeping beside me in our bed."

"I'm not going to have this conversation with you in front of our daughter."

"You had no problem telling her you couldn't stand being in the same house with me. If you're gonna tell it then tell it all. Don't hold nothing back!"

"Aaliyah, I'm sorry you have to hear this."

"Don't apologize for me!" My mother screamed out as she came closer to us. "You think you can't stand me! I can't stand you either! I'm so tired of being tired of you and your bullshit. I'm your wife. How long do you expect me to wait for you to decide to be my husband again?"

"Why can't you guys just make it work? I hate all this arguing! I can't remember the last time we've all been together happy as a family. I can't take it anymore!"

"Aaliyah, wait!" I heard my dad call out to me as I ran out the house but I kept going.

I got in my car and speeded off. It was too much for me to deal with. I didn't want to accept that my parent's marriage could be over. My mother told me so many times that he was her first true love, that what they shared was magical, a once in a lifetime type of love. With how they acted towards each other a few minutes ago, in my mind there was no way that could possibly be true.

I felt my phone vibrating and it was my dad calling me but I had nothing to say to him. Or maybe I was afraid of what he might say to me. It made me almost want to vomit at the thought of hearing him say the word divorce. Tears began trickling down my face. My cell began vibrating again and I looked down thinking it was my father calling back but instead it was Amir.

"Hello," I answered wanting to hear his voice.

"Aaliyah, what's wrong, are you ok?"

"No."

"What happened?"

"My parents just got in the biggest argument and I'm scared they're going to get a divorce." After I said the word out loud, the tears were no longer trickling they were rushing down my face.

"Aaliyah, calm down."

"I can't. The thought of my parents divorcing and Xavier growing up without my dad being around is too much for me to deal with."

"Just because your parents were arguing doesn't necessarily mean they're getting a divorce."

"You didn't see how ugly it got and it would've been worse if I wasn't there. Once I left, all hell probably broke loose."

"I hate for you to be this upset. I wish I was there with you."

"I do too."

"The summer will be here before you know it and we'll have a great time."

"I hope so."

"We will. Don't we always have fun when you come for the summer?"

"Yes," I answered with my voice cracking.

"Well this summer will be better than ever. We'll be high school graduates, preparing for college. We have the best years of our lives to look forward to."

"What if they don't make it, Amir?" my voice had turned completely serious.

"Aaliyah, you have to prepare yourself for that possibility. I hope it doesn't happen but it could. I have no idea what is going on with your mom and dad but I can promise you one thing."

"What's that?"

"No matter what, I'll be here to help you get through it. That's what best friends are for." After Amir said that I felt as if I could exhale.

"Thank you for that. I no longer feel alone in this."

"That's because you're not alone. We made a pact when we were little kids to always stand by each other's side through good, bad and ugly. I haven't forgotten and I take my pact seriously."

"You're so silly." We both started laughing.

"I'll admit I'm silly but I said something right because I got you smiling again."

"You did and I love you for it."

"I love you too. Now go do something fun. I'll talk to you later. Bye."

"Bye." Just like that Amir had me feeling good again. I felt so lucky to have him in my life. And although I was disappointed that he didn't give us a chance to be more than friends I realized his friendship was more important. I really did hope that he and Justina could make it as a couple because they both deserved to be happy and he truly was a great catch.

When I ended my phone call with Amir I was pulling up to D'Mario's condo. I glanced at the clock in my car and an hour and a half had passed since I spoke to him last. I knew he was furious but all I could say to myself was that shit happens.

I knocked at the door and waited a few seconds before ringing the doorbell. I knocked again and figured maybe he got so pissed with me that he hauled ass up outta there. I knocked one more time, and then decided to leave. When I was walking towards my car I heard the door open and D'Mario call out my name.

"I thought you had left."

"Nope, I fell asleep waiting on your slow ass," he grinned.

"Whatever, but I'm sorry about that. I had some problems at home."

"What sort of problems?" he asked closing the door behind me. I sat down on the cream leather sofa and let out a deep sigh.

"My parents are having some marital issues right now."

"That can't be good."

"It's not but it'll be ok."

"You seem to be handling it like a soldier."

"I wasn't at first but I talked to a good friend of mine and he made me feel a lot better."

"He, should I be jealous?"

"No. We're best friends, nothing more. He's actually Justina's boyfriend."

"Oh yeah, she broke my man's Ja Khel's heart when she told him she had a boyfriend."

"Every time we've gone out Ja Khel seems to be doing just fine. He's always with a different chick."

"I said she broke his heart not his dick."

"Yo, you're crazy."

"I'm saying. He did think she seemed like a nice girl. The type you can take home to meet your parents. I know you said yours are going through a tough time but I would still like to meet them. We've been seeing each other for some time now."

Deja King

"I haven't met your parents."

"That's because they live in Miami. But in a couple weeks I'm going there to visit. You need to make that trip with me."

"That sounds nice. But I'm not sure with school and all."

"We can go on a weekend so you won't have to miss school."

"True, but my parents might give me a hard time."

"That's why you should let me meet them so they can see who you've been spending all your time with. Is that a problem?" I didn't know if the expression on my face gave it away or if D'Mario could hear the hesitation in my voice. I wasn't in the mood to go there but I felt it was time to put it all on the table.

"Here's the thing, D'Mario. My parents don't know I'm seeing you."

"Why? What they don't allow you to date. They tryna make you a nun?"

"No. I never told you this but after our first date my mother forbad me to see you again."

"Why, she's never even met me."

"My grandfather who did meet you told her you were a drug dealer and that you weren't eighteen but twenty-two." D'Mario put his head down as if he was trying to get his thoughts together before defending himself.

"Both of those things are true but I guess you already knew that."

"Why did you lie to me about your age? I mean you had to know I was going to be suspicious. There

88

are a lot of rich kids in Beverly Hills but not many of them are living on their own in a super-hot condo with a couple of cars to drive."

"I figured you knew I wasn't really eighteen. That was more so me bullshitting than anything else. As far as my occupation go, again I figured you knew something was up but since you didn't press me about it I let it go."

"I was gonna let it go, but you was stressing me about meeting my family and I didn't know how to keep putting you off."

"At least now I understand why every time we go out you damn near be tryna have us in Calabasas. You want to make sure none of your people see us together."

I couldn't help but laugh because he was speaking the truth. For the last couple of months I would come up with every excuse in the book to get us as far away from Beverly Hills as possible. I didn't want to have another run in with my grandfather like before so I stayed extra cautious.

"I'm glad you find it funny."

"D'Mario, it's nothing personal against you. I really do have a good time when we're together, but my family is very protective."

"I can understand that. If you were my daughter I would be that way too. So what do you want to do?"

"You mean today?"

"That too, but I'm talking about us, our relationship. We can't stay in hiding forever unless you not tryna let things between us go any further."

"The whole drug dealer thing don't bother me. My family never talks about it but I ain't dumb. I know there are a lot of illegal activities that surround me and my people; I'm just sequestered from it. I'm eighteen now so I have every right to date you but I know it's going to be a problem and you may not be ready for that."

"What you mean?"

"I'm worried they may try to make your life difficult if they find out I've still been seeing you. I enjoy your company and I want us to have a good time, which means no complications."

"Ma, all I want to do is make you happy. No drama on my end," D'Mario said, putting his hand in the back pocket of my jeans and pulling me close to him.

"With those dimples and pretty white teeth, that's a good start to making me happy," I said kissing his soft lips. Dude was so fuckin' sexy and smelled so good. That was the main reason I kept dealing with him already knowing it wasn't in the cards for us. The more he hypnotized me with his scent and tongue the more I considered letting him be my first.

"You should let me bring you even more happiness," he teased, gently kissing on my earlobes.

"And how would you do that?"

"I can show you better than I can tell you." I looked up at the spiral staircase that led to the loft bedroom. I had been in there several times but I always made sure our bed contact was limited but for some reason today, I was feeling open to it. I think I wanted to feel good to take away feeling so bad about my parents.

"I'm hungry. Let's go get something to eat." I decided today wasn't the day I would get my cherry popped. As much as D'Mario turned me on, I wasn't ready to give up the goods just yet.

"So where do you want to go and have lunch—San Diego?"

"Oh, you got jokes."

"That's a reasonable question."

"No, we can get something right here in the neighborhood."

"You sure about that? Like you said, you don't want any complications."

"Fuck it, I need to live."

"Yeah, you do. There's so much I can show you, Aaliyah, if you let me."

"Can you show me how to make my own money?'

"Huh?"

"You heard me. Can you let me into your world so I can bring in my own paper?"

"Why would you need to do that? You come from a shit load of money."

"But it's not mine. I see myself out there buying shit and not having to go to my mommy and daddy to get it."

"How 'bout you come to me. I may not have the type of paper your family has but I'm also super straight."

"I believe that but I don't want that shit either. I mean I do want my man to be able to treat me right and show me a good time on his own dime but I want to be able to bring my own paper to the table."

"And you're willing to do some illegal shit to make that happen?"

"Why not, unless you're saying you ain't got nothing that I can do."

"Oh, I got something you can do. But is thrill seeking worth you risking your freedom."

"I'm not trying to be on the corner hustling. I won't get caught."

"Anytime you doing what I do there is a chance you can get caught no matter how slight it might be."

"I get it and I appreciate the warning but I think if I follow your lead I'll be good."

"Come on let's go. We can talk about your job description in the car." I grabbed my purse and followed D'Mario to his car.

It was gorgeous out so D'Mario drove his black convertible XK. When he put the top down and the breeze began hitting my face and blowing through my hair a renewed sense of happiness flooded over me. Being with D'Mario made me feel like a grown woman who could make her own decisions and do whatever the hell she wanted and I loved it.

"So where do you want to go eat?"

"It's up to you. I'm following your lead today."

"I like the way that sounds. But I want to go to this Italian restaurant about ten minutes away. Are you cool with that?"

I lowered my shades so D'Mario could see my eyes, "Like I said, I'm following your lead."

"Only checking. But one of the reasons I like it is because it's a low key spot. If you want to go someplace and not be seen, this is the place."

"Whatever. I'm relaxed and this breeze is feeling so good and I'm loving your car. I need to get me a convertible."

"Yeah, everybody needs a convertible in their collection."

"So this and the Range are the only cars you have?"

"Nope, I actually have four. I keep the other two at my crib in Miami."

"Let me guess they're black?" I smiled.

D'Mario turned and looked at me with a grin and replied, "Yes."

"It's obvious black is your favorite color. You always wear black. Everything in your condo is basically black except for the cream sofa and some of the other décor. You even wear black diamonds."

"You got a problem with that?"

"No, I think it's sexy." When we got to the red light I leaned over and kissed D'Mario. He was irresistible to me. And the fact that dude made his paper the illegal way instead of sitting in an office doing a nine to five turned me on for some reason.

"And you're sexy to me too. That's why it's getting more and more difficult for me not being able to have my way with you. I mean you let me touch but you never let me explore. How long you gon' make a nigga wait?"

"I haven't decided yet."

"Excuse me?"

"You heard me. I haven't decided yet. It's gon' happen but when I'm not sure. But you'll be the second to know."

"You a funny one, but I like it. No worries I've waited this long I can wait some more, plus you worth it."

"D'Mario, you act like you've been holding out for

over a year, it's only been a few months."

"True, but it feels like so much longer. I mean damn, look at you! Even right now you got on that short, what type of dress is this," he said grabbing the bottom of it.

"It's called a baby doll dress."

"Yep, and you looking just like a doll. This dress shows enough to turn a nigga on but not too much so you also make a nigga curious what's under it. How do you expect me to not want to get closer to you?"

"I get it and all that will happen in due time."

"I thought you said you were following my lead today."

"Oh, I didn't mention that certain restrictions apply." We both laughed as D'Mario parked the car so we could go inside. We were dead in the middle of Beverly Hills holding hands walking in the restaurant like we were a couple and for that brief moment I didn't care who saw. I think watching my parent's marriage ending right before my eyes and being rejected by Amir made me want to rebel against everything that was supposed to be right.

I couldn't front for the first couple months it crushed me that Amir had chosen Justina over me. Although I had always been super attracted to D'Mario, I kinda threw myself in this thing with him to help get over the disappointment of Amir not wanting me but as time went on I had developed real feelings for him. So now I no longer had to listen to Justina gush over her boyfriend, I had one too, except he was a man and not a boy.

When we walked in the quaint Italian restaurant the first thing I noticed was that Ja Khel was coming towards us. But to my surprise he wasn't totting some arm candy along he had a guy with him.

"What's up man, hey Aaliyah."

"Hey, Ja Khel." I was too busy eyeing the guy he was with to really pay attention to Ja Khel. The guy seemed familiar to me for some reason.

"I thought you said you were laying low today."

"I planned to but Aaliyah got hungry," he said squeezing my hand playfully. "Aaliyah, this quiet dude with Ja Khel is my brother Darius." *Now I understood why he seemed familiar to me he looked like D'Mario but a more mature version,* I thought to myself.

"It's good to meet you." He remained mute and just nodded his head.

"So are ya'll staying or leaving?"

"We on our way out."

"Cool, I'll call you later. We have a few things to discuss." D'Mario watched as they made their exit out before we followed the hostess to our table.

"So when are we going to discuss what I brought up to you earlier?"

"Ma, I got you. I have to find the right thing for you to do. But on the real I'm hoping you'll change your mind."

"Why would you hope that for?"

"Because you one of those rich girls looking for a good time. Ain't nothing good about this shit but the money."

"Yeah, and it must be nice to have a bunch of it

and not have to ask nobody for nothing."

"Everybody answer to somebody, Aaliyah. I don't care how high up they are, there is always somebody higher."

"I hear a sermon 'bout to come from you so let's order our food and move to another topic."

"I'm not tryna preach and it sound like you catching an attitude."

"No attitude. I'm just not interested in you trying to give me some long drawn out story to change my mind. If you not gon' do it, say that and then let's move on."

"You so fuckin' feisty."

"I know. So what's good on the menu? I'm ready to eat."

I had to end that going nowhere conversation with D'Mario before he got me livid. I understood if he didn't want me involved in his illegal activities because there were valid reasons to be concerned but what I wasn't interested in was a lecture. I got enough of them from my parents and my grandfather. I would continue to have fun with D'Mario but I knew there was no chance we would ever be Bonnie and Clyde.

"I can't believe in a few months we'll be done with high school. And then I can go spend the summer with my baby."

"So I take it things are still going good with you and Amir?"

"Not good, great! We finally did it and it was amazing!" My upper body lifted up so quickly off the chaise lounge when I heard what Justina said that I almost dropped my strawberry daiquiri.

"When you said did it are you talking about sex?"

"Keep your voice down. My nosey mother might be lurking around somewhere."

"We're outside by the pool, she's in the house. I doubt she can hear what we're saying."

"Trust me her hearing is exceptional. Ask my dad. He's been caught creepin' more than a couple of times for that very reason."

"Fine," I said lowering my voice. "You and Amir had sex?"

"No, we made love and it was beautiful. We did it when I went to visit him for Christmas break. If I'd known the sex would be that incredible I wouldn't have waited at all. The size of his dick is like ridiculous. But it's not like it's so big he'll rip your insides up. That's just disgusting."

"I can't believe you're just now telling me. I also can't believe you had sex before me. I'm probably like the only eighteen year old virgin in Beverly Hills."

"You're still a virgin?"

"Isn't that what I just said and there's no need to rub it in."

"I wasn't trying to rub it in. I was under the impression that you and D'Mario had been having sex. I mean you're with him all the time."

"We mess around but never all the way."

"What are you waiting for?"

"I don't know."

"Well you better hurry up. A guy that fine is definitely getting it in with somebody."

"As long as I don't know about it, it's not my problem. Plus, I'm not about to fuck D'Mario because I'm afraid he's getting pussy from some other chick. If that's what he wants to do, it will happen regardless if we're having sex or not."

"I think it's important to please your man. I've been practicing on a banana how to give Amir the perfect blow job."

"You can't be serious. A fuckin' banana, Justina. That's like the lamest shit I've ever heard."

"Call it lame if you want but my man ain't complaining and that's all that matters."

I laid down and put my sunglasses back on so Justina couldn't see the loathing in my eyes. It was like she thought she was such hot shit because of her relationship with Amir. And now that they were fucking, you couldn't tell her nothing. But I could lie to Justina but I couldn't lie to myself. There was a twinge of jealousy burning inside of me. She got the man and he popped her cherry. I was tired of being the hottest virgin running around here. I made up my mind that before high school ended the word 'virgin' would no longer be a part of my description.

After leaving Justina's house I headed over to D'Mario's crib. He cooked some of his mouth watering Salmon that I simply adored. My stomach was fixated on how good I knew that food would taste but my mind kept replaying what Justina had revealed to me earlier when we were lounging by the pool. As I drove with the windows down and the nighttime air blowing in my face I wondered if I would find a guy that made me as happy as Amir made Justina. D'Mario was super cool and sexy as all get out but I knew he wasn't 'the one'. But I guess he would have to do for now, I resolved myself to accept that as I drove up in his condo complex. When I got out the car, D'Mario was outside on the phone pacing back and forth. When he realized I was walking up he nodded his head telling me to go inside. There was soft music playing and our dinner was laid out real elegantly on the dining room table with flowers and candles. It was sophisticated but sexy at the same time. I was glad that I had on a cute silk dress so it seemed I was dressed appropriately for the occasion. When I sat down at the table the candles made the low cut neckline embellished with sparkling beads and stones appear to illuminate.

I continued to sit at the table waiting patiently for D'Mario to come back in but the time was ticking away. I wanted us to share this moment together but I was starving so I began devouring my Salmon. He put some sort of special sauce on it that he refused to share with me which made this the best piece of fish I had ever tasted in my entire life. By the time I was halfway done, D'Mario still hadn't come back inside so it was a clear indication I made the right decision eating my food instead of waiting for him.

"Damn, you ate already," he said with a borderline frown on his face when he walked back in as I was finishing up my last few bites.

"I tried to wait but you were out there forever. You see what time it is."

"Fuck, I didn't realize I was on the phone for that long," he said looking at the clock on his wall."

"Why were you talking outside anyway?"

"This a bullshit phone and I can't really get no reception in here."

"Oh, I know you're ready to eat. Do you want me to warm up your food for you?"

"No, I lost my fuckin' appetite."

"Does it have anything to do with that phone conversation you just had?"

"Everything."

"Tell me what happened." D'Mario looked away from me as if resisting the urge to spill the details. "You can talk to me. I am your girlfriend...right?"

"Really, you tell me."

"What is that supposed to mean?"

"I've been wanting you to be my girlfriend for a while now. But I feel like you fighting against it."

"That's not true."

"One minute you seem all in it then the next you easing back. So I'm not sure if you're my girlfriend or not."

"I'm telling you I am. I mean if that's something you still want." D'Mario walked over to an end table in the hallway and opened the drawer. He pulled out a long black box.

"I've been wanting to give you this," he said handing the box to me." When I opened the box my mouth dropped.

"Omifuckingoodness! You got me Lorraine Schwartz jewelry. These earrings cost like twenty-five thousand dollars. I know this because a few weeks ago I went shopping with my mother and she was contemplating getting them but didn't. I can't believe you bought them for me, they're beautiful. Thank you so much!" I stood up and put the 4"18k YG and Briolette Diamond earrings on. My jet black curls fell perfectly to make them sparkle even more.

"I take it that you like them."

"You knew I would fuckin' love them. Who wouldn't! How long have you had them and why are you just now giving them to me?"

"For a couple weeks. I didn't want you to think I was trying to buy you in order to make you mine."

"I wouldn't have thought that."

"You're so hard to read, Aaliyah. The only reason I knew you wanted to be my girl is because of what you said a minute ago. You never gave me any indication you wanted us to be exclusive."

"Well I do and if you keep giving me jewelry like this I might be trying to move in."

"Don't say it unless you mean it. I don't think you understand how much I'm into you." D'Mario tugged me closer, kissing me. "And those earrings look beautiful on you."

"Thank you. And thank you for having such amazing taste in jewelry. Now that you're feeling more relaxed will you tell me what had you so upset."

D'Mario rubbed his hand over his face. The loving

smile that he had a second ago vanished and a look of skepticism now etched his face. "A problem came up and it got me concerned."

"Tell me what the problem is."

"For the last year every other week this guy that works for me goes to Culver City and meets my main connect. All he does is pickup an envelope that has a key in it and the location of my product, because my connect switches it up each time. But for some reason dude has vanished and tomorrow is the pickup."

"What do you mean vanished?"

"He's disappeared."

"When was the last time you spoke to him?"

"Earlier in the week but he ain't answering his phone, he ain't at his crib. Not only am I worried about getting that envelope tomorrow but I'm also worried about dude. He's good people"

"Why don't you just go get the envelope?"

"Nah. I've only met with my connect one time in person. He prefers we always use an in-between in case somebody is watching. It's worked so far so I wanna keep it like that and I don't want to piss my connect off 'cause he mad paranoid."

"I'm sure you know somebody that can go in that other guys place."

"Nobody that I trust a hundred percent. You have to understand, the person that gets that envelope has access to my drugs before I do. People out here thirsty right now. I can't take those types of chances."

"Why don't you call the guy and reschedule."

"He don't fuck wit' the phone. If somebody don't

show up tomorrow to get that envelope he might think some funny shit is up and cut me off. That's why I'm stressing."

"I can go." D'Mario raised his head up and from the look he gave me I knew he was unconvinced. "You need somebody to go, and I can do it. It's a one time thing and you can trust me."

"I don't know, Aaliyah," D'Mario said, shaking his head as he stood up from the chair.

"Real talk, it's not like you have any other options. Unless you're willing to lose your connect."

"Are you sure you're comfortable with this?"

"All I'm doing is picking up an envelope."

"Yeah, a very important envelope."

"Yep, and I'll do my job very well since I know I'll be well compensated for it."

"Excuse me?"

"What do you mean excuse me? You didn't think I was doing it for free. I'm sure your little dude that's missing got paid and so will I."

"Can't dispute that. This can work and if dude stay missing, it'll give me two weeks to find a replacement."

"Yep, so it's a win, win situation." D'Mario didn't know it but I hoped the replacement would be me. I could see myself making this a permanent gig. Getting paid easy money to go pick up an envelope and if I played my cards right I could parlay it into something much bigger.

Amir

Let It Go

When I saw my dad and Nico pulling up I thought I would feel a sense of relief but I didn't. Their arrival simply made me more anxious. My dad got out the car first and walked over to me while Nico was on the phone.

"What took you so long to get here?" I could tell my dad didn't appreciate the tone of my question but he didn't address it. Probably because he knew it was due to my frustration over Aaliyah.

"When we got the call we were in Long Island and the traffic was horrible. What the hell happened?"

"I don't know. I was hoping you all had the answers. I've been in my car waiting. Nobody in the precinct is telling me anything."

"Nico is on the phone with his attorney so hopefully we'll know soon."

"What I do know is they're charging her with murder."

"Yeah, first degree. Here comes Nico now, maybe the attorney gave him some more information."

"Hey, Amir."

"Hey, did you find out anything?"

"Not really. My attorney said they're on some real secretive bullshit right now. He's in LA but he's getting on a redeye so he can handle things on Aaliyah's behalf. Amir, you wait here. Genesis, come with me inside and let's see what we can find out."

"I wanna come," I uttered more aggressively than I meant to.

"Do like Nico asked and wait here. We'll be back." The tenor in my father's voice let me know the request wasn't up for debate. I literally kicked rocks trying to find a way to release my irritation. I had been waiting all this time and the last thing I wanted to do was wait some more. I wanted to be inside and find out what was going on with Aaliyah. But instead I found myself back in my car remembering how things were already becoming complicated only a few months ago.

"So exactly what are we going to do while you're here? I know you and your boo want to spend some alone time together but hopefully we can all do some fun things together too," Aaliyah smiled as we drove down Mulholland Drive.

"Of course we're going to all hang out, that's why I'm here. We celebrating my birthday so all we doing is fun shit."

"I'm glad you came to the west coast to celebrate."

"You all couldn't make it to New York and I had a couple days off from school so why not. I needed some

LA fresh air anyway," which was true. As many times as I came to the west coast, I never grew tired of driving down Mulholland Dr. at night, gazing at the Santa Monica Mountains and the panoramic views of LA, including the Hollywood Sign.

"Yeah, there's no place like LA except New York which beats everything. I wish I could have some of their pizza right now."

"Yo, why you even mention pizza 'cause I'm starving."

"Me too. I have the perfect place for us to go. There's this Italian spot right in Beverly Hills. The food is off the chain. D'Mario and I go all the time. Let's go there."

"That works. Let's go. Speaking of D'Mario how's that working out?"

"It's working out good. You see these earrings I have on, he got them for me."

"For real! Them shits look mad pricey."

"They are. They cost like twenty-five g's."

"Get the fuck outta here! What that nigga do?"

"He's a drug dealer. That's why I'm keeping the relationship on the low because my mother already told me to stay away from him."

"How did she find out he's a drug dealer."

"My grandfather snitched."

"Leave it up to Quentin to try and spoil your fun but you know he means well. He love him some Aaliyah."

"Shut up!"

"You know I'm telling the truth. So when am I going to meet your boyfriend?"

"We should all go out to dinner while you're here. That'll be nice. D'Mario's been dying to know who the hell is this Amir cat I always be talking about. Now he can find out."

"So how serious are things between you two?"

"He's like my first real boyfriend so serious enough."

"Have you guys, you know..."

"Are you asking me if we've had sex yet?"

"Nope. So that makes me the only virgin in the clique because I know you and Justina have been getting it in for a minute now."

"She told you?"

"Of course! She couldn't wait to tell me how amazing the sex was."

"I'm sorry you had to hear that."

"Don't be sorry. I'm good with you all's relationship now. D'Mario makes me happy. So I guess you can say I'm over that crush or whatever you want to call it that I had on you."

"That's good to hear and I'm glad you've moved on and happy with D'Mario," I lied. Call me selfish but I didn't want Aaliyah to get over whatever it was that she felt for me. In my mind she was mine.

"We're here."

"Damn, this shit is in the cut."

"I know," Aaliyah laughed. "When D'Mario first took me here he said if you wanted to creep and not be seen this was the spot to go to. But wait till you eat the food, it's so delicious."

"As hungry as I am anything would be good," I said holding the door open as Aaliyah and I walked inside.

"Tell the hostess to get us a table because I can't eat anything until I go to the bathroom. I'll be right back."

"Cool." I wasted no time getting to the hostess. "Let me get a table for two."

"Sure, do you want to be seated now or wait for your guest?"

"You can go ahead and seat me and when she comes out the bathroom, bring her to our table."

"No problem, follow me." While trailing behind the hostess the moonlight coming through the window shined on a couple in the back corner. Their deep, intense kissing got my attention. As my eyes zoomed on them closer my mouth dropped. I immediately turned around and made my way back to the front. I knew the hostess was going to wonder what the hell happened to me but I didn't care. I was rushing so quickly that I ended up bumping right into Aaliyah.

"Amir, where are you going?"

"I changed my mind. I don't have the taste for Italian food. Let's go someplace else."

"I promise you; once you taste the food you're going to love it. Now come on, I don't feel like going somewhere else," Aaliyah said grabbing my arm. Before I could stop her, that same moonlight that stopped me in my tracks had the exact same affect on her.

"Aaliyah, I'm sorry. I didn't want you to see that."

"This can't be happening." I could see the tears swell up in her eyes and it was breaking my heart.

"Let's go. You can deal with it later."

"No, I'ma deal with it right now." Aaliyah stormed off and I was right behind her.

"Please don't let this turn ugly," I whispered under my breath.

"This is where you've been sneaking off to!"

"Aaliyah, what are you doing here?"

"The question is what are you doing here? You're in a restaurant tonguing down some other man! How could you do this to me!"

"Keep your voice down."

"Who is he? Wait you're that man that I met at Amir's house. You're Genesis's friend."

"Aaliyah, stop it."

"No mother, you stop it! How could you do this? Have you been having an affair with him since back then? That was months ago." Aaliyah's voice was so loud that people in the restaurant were now staring in our direction trying to see what was going on. None of us needed that type of attention so I decided to try again to get Aaliyah to leave.

"Aaliyah, we need to go."

"Did you know about this and not tell me?"

"Of course not! I had no idea that your mom and Lorenzo were seeing each other."

"Don't lie to me, Amir."

"I'm not. Now let's go. We can talk about this in the car."

"Aaliyah, Amir is right. Let's discuss this outside." With reluctance Aaliyah followed her mom outside and I sat down with Lorenzo.

"You don't owe me an explanation but I need to know, does my dad know about this?"

"Yes, I told him a few weeks ago. I hate that you

and Aaliyah had to find out like this."

"She's married and Aaliyah is Nico's daughter but I'm not telling you nothing that you don't already know. No disrespect but this some messy shit."

"None taken and you're absolutely right. Trust me I didn't plan to fall for her but I did."

"What you tryna say that ya'll in love? What part don't you get, she's married."

"Oh, I get that."

"You just don't care. I know Nico doesn't know."

"Of course not."

"How do adults expect for kids to make the right decisions when they can't make it their damn selves. Great fuckin' example you guys are," I groaned getting up from the table.

"Amir, wait."

"What is it?"

"I like you. You're an exceptional young man. Don't let this define our relationship."

"I hear you, Lorenzo, but I need to go check on Aaliyah." When I got outside Aaliyah and her mom were in the parking lot exchanging heated words. That was better than what I imagined it would be. As I got up closer on them I could hear what was being said and to my surprise Precious was not backing down.

"Aaliyah, of course this isn't how I wanted you to find out about Lorenzo but I'm not going to apologize to you for finding some happiness and holding on to it."

"You make it seem like there is no happiness left with daddy."

"What house have you been living in?" Precious

asked sarcastically. "There isn't any happiness left in my marriage and hasn't been for a very long time and you know that."

"But you don't throw your family away for some meaningless affair."

"It's not meaningless. Lorenzo is very important to me."

"Are you saying you're going to leave daddy for him?"

"I don't know but it's my decision to make and I would appreciate it if you give me that."

"Is that what you call a polite way of asking me not to expose your affair?"

"Yes it is. Until you get married and you're able to survive the good, bad and the ugly, hold off on being judgmental."

"Fine, I'll keep your little secret but while you're contemplating whether to fight for your marriage, think about Xavier. I'm eighteen so I'll get over it. But Xavier is just a kid who needs his mother and father together. So while you're in that restaurant tonguing down Lorenzo, think about that. Let's go, Amir."

"Goodnight," I said to Precious before following Aaliyah back to her car. The entire situation was fucked up but I didn't think Precious or Lorenzo were bad people they just made a bad decision they would no doubt cause even greater consequences.

"I can't believe this shit! Amir, you promise you didn't know about this?" Aaliyah asked me again when we got in the car.

"I promise. Why is it so hard for you to believe

me?"

"Your dad and Lorenzo are close. I would think your dad would've mentioned it to you."

"So would I but he didn't. Maybe he didn't want to put me in the middle of it. He knew I would feel obligated to tell you."

"Then why were you trying to get me out the restaurant and hide it from me?"

"Because exactly what I was trying to avoid, happened. I didn't want you and your mother having a blowout in the middle of a fuckin' restaurant. When I saw them together my first reaction was to protect you and that meant not letting you see it. But once I got you far away from there I had every intention of letting you know."

"I apologize for doubting you."

"You don't have to. I know how fucked up you're feeling right now. They not even my parents and I'm feeling fucked up. Then I'm thinking about Nico."

"What about my dad?"

"Lorenzo is doing business with him. I don't know how long that will last once he finds out."

"Do you think I should tell him?"

"Hell No! This shit is fucked up but like my dad would say, this grown folks business and stay the fuck out of it."

"But it isn't right. Lorenzo is fucking my mother but then doing business with my dad."

"See I shouldn't have even said anything. In all honesty the shit is actually separate. Lorenzo's personal life doesn't have anything to do with his business. It's not like your mother is married to Nico and Lorenzo stepped in and started having an affair with her."

"So now you're defending him!"

"All I'm trying to say is that I don't believe Lorenzo was trying to slight Nico so don't tell your dad, either one of them. Let your mother handle this. Trust me everything will come to the light without you even putting your two cents in...it always does."

"Fine, I won't say anything."

"You give me your word?"

"Yes, I put that on our friendship. But hopefully my mother realizes her marriage is worth saving and ends that bullshit relationship with Lorenzo. You know what's crazy about this?"

"What?"

"My mom and dad constantly argued over Nico. My dad just knew there was something going on between them. How ironic is it that he's not even the one my mother turned to."

After Aaliyah said that, we both remained silent for the duration of the car ride. Our appetites were now nonexistent and all we both wanted to do was go home. This shit had ruined our evening and I hoped it wasn't a precursor for how the rest of my birthday weekend would go.

"You are still coming tomorrow?" I questioned Aaliyah before getting out her car to go in the house.

"Of course. I wouldn't miss your birthday party for nothing. You always come through for me."

"And I always will." I gave Aaliyah a kiss on her cheek and went in the house. I knew a birthday party wouldn't make Aaliyah forget what went down tonight but maybe some fun would be an excellent deviation.

When I entered the house, from the two story circular entry I could see my dad pouring himself a drink at the bar. "Amir, will you come here," he yelled out from the living room.

I was in no rush to get to my dad so instead I did a mental tour of our new house in order to slow down my pace. I already knew what he wanted to discuss and I was a tad dismayed with him for not telling me about Lorenzo and Precious. I was hoping by the time I made it to him some of that anger would've subsided. So I stared up at the sky-high ceilings, admired the glided moldings and massive fireplace and even complimented how stunning the chandeliers were in my mind. "What is it?"

"Lorenzo called and told me what happened," my dad stated, getting straight to the point.

"Yeah it got ugly real quick."

"How's Aaliyah doing?"

"Not good. She thought I knew what was going on between them and didn't tell her?"

"You explained to her you didn't."

"Of course but I would've known if you had told me."

"I knew it would be a mistake. You would've felt compelled to tell Aaliyah and I couldn't let that happen."

"That didn't work out because now she knows."

"Were you able to convince her to stay quiet about what she knows?"

"I think so."

"That's not good enough."

"She gave me her word but I can't control what she does."

"The two of you are very close. You need to make sure she understands how important it is that she keeps what she knows to herself."

"I did but understandably she's hurt."

"And we all regret that but this has to be handled delicately."

"You mean because of Nico."

"Yes. We're running a lucrative business and unfortunately I'm afraid that Nico won't be able to separate the business from the personal."

"You always taught me that was the number one rule in this game."

"It is but everybody has that one person in their life that the rule doesn't apply to and for Nico it's Precious."

"Maybe you should've informed Lorenzo of that before he took Precious to bed." My dad began shaking the ice cubes in his glass around before pouring himself another drink. I knew that meant he was trying not to let his temper get the best of him.

"Son, I can appreciate that you're upset that Aaliyah has been hurt by what her mother and Lorenzo are doing but it is happening and from what they both told me it's not going to stop anytime soon. So we have to find the best way to deal with it. Right now that means everybody remaining silent, including you."

"Aaliyah already knows who else would I tell?"

"Your girlfriend Justina."

"I comprehend the importance of silence."

"Excellent because you've been asking me for a very long time to let you be a part of the organization and loyalty to our business is essential. If you can't keep your emotions under control it won't work."

"I told you I was ready and I am. I'm fully aware of the rules and I'll follow them."

"That's what I needed to hear," my dad said nodding his head and loosening the tie on his white shirt. "Are you ready for your party tomorrow?" switching the subject quickly was my dad's way of saying that the other conversation was over without actually saying it.

"Yes I am. I'm finally eighteen about to graduate and move on to the next phase of my life. Having a big celebration is a great way to start it off."

"I think you and everybody else will have a wonderful time. Get some rest tonight you have a big day tomorrow."

"Will do. Goodnight, dad."

"Goodnight." No matter how calm and in control my dad conducted himself there was no denying this affair that Lorenzo and Precious were having was stressing him out. I'm sure it had been from the moment he found out. Now with Aaliyah in the loop that brought another element of tension. He knew I could be trusted but he didn't hold the same assurance in Aaliyah but only time would tell.

I stood at the top of the double adjoining spiral

stairwell and watched as the guest arrived to my birthday party. My dad really went all out to make sure he exceeded my expectations. A selected few of friends that I went to school with in New York were flown in and so were my grandmother and grandfather from my mother's side. My eyes lit up when Justina walked in with her parents wearing a mini-slit white dress. Each time I saw her it seemed she was getting sexier with her appearance. As if she could feel me lusting after her she glanced up smiling and waving at me. I gestured my hand for her to come up and she said a few words to her parents and hurried up the stairs. I greeted her at the top giving her a wet kiss.

"You look unfuckin' believable tonight."

"My dad almost had a seizure when I came out my bedroom. He tried to bribe me to change my outfit but it was more important to me to give you a hard-on when you saw me than anything he was offering."

"You made the right choice because all I want to do right now is take you in my bedroom. I can't wait for you to see it. It's bigger than a one bedroom New York City apartment and it has panoramic views of the entire Los Angeles Basin.

"So what are we waiting for?" I couldn't help but smile at Justina's question.

"It's not time yet, baby. But before the nights over I'm going to make sure you give me my birthday present."

"No worries by me because I'm going to make sure I do too. I already know where we'll be spending the majority of our time while you're here," she teased kissing my neck.

"Are you trying to get me to fuck you right here on the stairs."

"That would be sexy, especially in this house. Did I mention how gorgeous this place is? I remember you telling me your dad was buying a house on the west coast but I didn't know he was getting a European styled mansion in Holmby Hills."

"I was as shocked as you when he first showed it to me. He always claimed we were bachelors and didn't need a huge house. I guess he changed his mind."

"He beyond changed his mind. He went to the complete left. When my dad was driving up that long winding cobblestone driveway and my mom saw the motor court that look like it could fit a zillion cars she told my dad she wanted a new house because this one made her feel poor."

"Your mother has always been dramatic."

"True but she's right this place is gorgeous and you're in the perfect location. With Aaliyah living in Beverly Hills, me in Bel-Air and you in Holmby Hills we're representing what they call the "Platinum Triangle" of Los Angeles."

"Is that what they call it?"

"Yep! Now that your dad bought this amazing place, maybe you should consider going to college out here."

"I love LA but I'm an east coast New York type of dude. Maybe you should consider going to school in NYC. Aaliyah is and if you come the clique will be there and we can run New York."

"My mother wants me here but I'm working on it because there is no place I would rather be than with you."

"I can't believe they came together," I mumbled under my breath getting distracted.

"What did you say?"

"I said I wondered when Aaliyah would get here since her parents just came in."

"Together?"

"Yeah, why do you say it like that?" I was checking to see if Aaliyah couldn't hold it in and confided everything to Justina.

"Aaliyah told me a few weeks ago their marriage was in serious trouble so I'm surprised they came together. But maybe they're trying to work it out, which would be great for Aaliyah and especially her brother."

"I hope they are trying to work it out too," I said gazing off as my mind was about to go into deep thought before getting interrupted by Justina's loud outburst.

"No she fuckin' didn't!"

"Lower your voice. No who fuckin' didn't?" my eyes followed the direction Justina was staring at and there was Aaliyah. "Who's that man she's with?"

"D'Mario. Is she trying to get her mother to kill her tonight?" My mind instantly went back to last night when Aaliyah told me about her boyfriend and how her mother didn't approve because he was a drug dealer.

"Let's go," I said taking Justina's hand and going downstairs.

"You mean let's go save Aaliyah because she's going to need it." By the time we got to the bottom stair,

Aaliyah was greeting us with her boyfriend.

"Hey you guys. D'Mario, you already know Justina but this is Amir."

"How you doing, Aaliyah is always saying positive things about you. Good to finally put a face to a name."

"It's good to meet you too." Before I could say anything else, Justina jumped in with her warning.

"Here comes trouble." We all turned around and saw Precious and Supreme coming in our direction. I hadn't seen them in the presence of each other for so long that I had forgotten how perfect they looked together. Although Supreme was no longer a superstar rapper he still carried himself with the confidence and swagger of a multi-platinum artist. And Precious was no doubt an undeniable beauty who had just enough toughness and mystic that kept you drawn to her. I understood why she was involved in a love triangle. She was wearing a canary yellow floor length dress with a high slit and a pair of nude pumps that made her legs appear endless. I had to admit she almost had me salivating.

"Hey mom and dad, this is D'Mario."

"Nice to meet you, Mr. and Mrs. Mills." Supreme extended his hand so clearly he didn't know his occupation but the look on Precious's face was priceless.

"Mom, aren't you going to speak," Aaliyah gloated, knowing the ball was in her court.

"Hello, D'Mario. Aaliyah failed to mention she was bringing you tonight."

"I didn't think it was necessary. I knew you wouldn't have a problem with it," Aaliyah smiled trying her best to get under her mother's skin and it damn sure was working because the frown hadn't left her face yet.

"D'Mario, it was good meeting you and hopefully we'll see you again."

"You will, daddy."

"Thank you, Sir. It was an honor to meet you and you too, Mrs. Mills."

"Come on, Precious, I see a business associate I want to introduce you to."

"Coming, Supreme, and we'll talk later." Precious let it be known that mother and daughter had unfinished business to deal with.

"That was awkward! How in the hell did you get your mother not to slap the shit out of you right here in the middle of this party." Aaliyah eyed me and I discreetly shook my head letting her know not to even think about coming clean to Justina.

"I'm eighteen now and decided it was time I took a stand."

"And...because that can't possibly be it."

"Justina, can we talk about this later. It's a party remember, we're supposed to be celebrating."

"True! Amir, let's go out by the pool. I always forget her name but I heard your dad has that new hot artist performing. We gotta catch that."

"You guys go ahead. I need to run something by Aaliyah right quick." I peeped the angst on Justina's face so I cleaned it up. "It's about a surprise I'm planning for you."

"Okay then," Justina beamed. "Come on, D'Mario I'll introduce you to some people."

"What the hell were you thinking?" I laid into

Aaliyah as soon as they were out of earshot. "I don't appreciate you using my party to make this round two with your mother."

"Relax, we didn't argue."

"Only because your mother played it cool instead of going upside your head. You told me last night that she said you couldn't see D'Mario anymore months ago. So to spit in her face you bring him to this party."

"Why is it that you always seem to defend everybody else but me?"

"Because sometimes, Aaliyah, you act like such a fuckin' brat. This isn't a competition with your mother of you hurt me so I'm gonna hurt you back."

"That's not what I'm doing."

"Yes the fuck it is and you need to stop, now."

"She doesn't want me dating D'Mario because he's a drug dealer yet she's having an affair. What type of hypocritical shit is that? She's in no position to judge my boyfriend when she can't even honor the vows she took in marriage."

"Even if your point is valid, this isn't how you present it."

"Whatever, Amir. You're never on my side so I don't care what you think."

"This bullshit attitude you have is the main reason I decided not to fuck with you and make it work with Justina. It always has to be about you."

"Well thank you for clearing that up. Now excuse me, my boyfriend is waiting for me."

I was furious at myself for losing my cool. I needed to speak with my father to get some advice on how to fix shit with Aaliyah. As I strolled through the party searching for him, I noticed he was standing in the entrance of the library with my Aunt Nichelle, some young lady that looked familiar like I had seen her in a music video or something and Lorenzo who was leaning against one of the marble columns. They appeared to be in an intense discussion and I didn't want to interrupt. It did puzzle me what that particular group of people could be discussing that required such seriousness. The match up seemed off.

"There you are." Justina snuck up behind me wrapping her arms around my waist. "What are you doing over here by yourself?"

"I needed to speak to my dad but he seems to be in the middle of something serious so I'm waiting for him to finish things up."

"I see. I tried to get Aaliyah to tell me what that surprise was that you were planning for me but she was so tight lipped. I couldn't get anything out of her. Now I'm going to work on getting it out of you."

"Justina, if I tell you then it won't be a surprise, now will it?"

"Surprises are overrated. I want to know."

"Give me a second. I think my dad is done over there and what I have to talk to him about can't wait. I'll be back."

"Okay, and I guess I'll be waiting."

"Don't pout. I'll make it up to you," I promised giving Justina a quick kiss. I raced over to my dad because I knew it was only a matter of seconds before somebody else would be up in his face wanting to have a discussion with him. "Dad," I called out to get his attention before somebody else did.

"Amir, I was just asking Nichelle where you were."

"I saw you guys over here but didn't want to interrupt."

"You know she started her modeling agency a few months ago."

"Yes, I remember when she was looking for an office space."

"Well Lorenzo knows a young lady that has some modeling experience but needs someone to guide her and give her that big break into the business. So we introduced her to Nichelle. We think it's a perfect fit."

"Is she going to sign her up?"

"Yes, she is, but enough about that. I'm sure that's not the reason you were tracking me down."

"No, it's about Aaliyah."

"Dammit, did she say something already?"

"No, but now I'm wondering how long that will last."

"Why, did something else happen?"

"Yes, she showed up at the party with a boyfriend she knows her mother doesn't approve of. Then she rubbed it in Precious's face as if daring her to go against it in front of Supreme."

"How did Precious handle it?"

"Surprisingly well unlike me. I ripped into Aaliyah for acting so immature and now she's pissed at me. How do you think I can smooth things over?"

"Amir, women are all delicate, I don't care how strong they appear. You have to move with caution when dealing with them so pointing out Aaliyah's immaturity under these circumstances is counterproductive."

"I know that, that's why I'm coming to you."

"Are you in love with, Aaliyah?"

"Where did that come from...no. I'm in love with Justina," I stuttered being taken off guard with the question.

"I was only checking."

"Now that we got that out the way are you going to tell me how I can make this right? If Aaliyah doesn't feel she can confide in me I'm worried she might act out."

"And start telling people about Lorenzo and Precious."

"Exactly."

"The only thing I can suggest is speak to Aaliyah from the heart."

"Huh?"

"You heard me. Be honest. Only you know how you feel and why. So tell her."

"That's it?"

"That's all you need. If you take my advice that will be enough to convince her to keep her word and not say anything about her mother and Lorenzo."

"I hope you're right."

"I am. Now go handle this thing with Aaliyah because time isn't on your side." When my dad walked away I stood and considered what he said. How could something so simple feel so complicated? Maybe there was a part of me that feared the truth but that was all going to change tonight.

I headed outside towards the pool pavilion and from the distance I could see Aaliyah and D'Mario by the hillsides that was filled with orchids. They were holding hands and kissing each other like they were in love. He kept sliding his hand up her white and pink spotted mini dress then she would playfully slap it away. As I got closer they disappeared into the cabana and my mind began visualizing all the things they were about to do to each other and it made my stomach knot up. I turned away and decided the truth about my feelings towards Aaliyah would stay with me.

Aaliyah

The Best I Never Had

As the hours dwindled by, I regretted that the one phone call I was able to make was to my mother. She or nobody else had shown up yet and so of course I blamed her. I was wondering after we hung up did she say fuck me and go back to sleep. I couldn't think of any reason why either one of my dad's or my grandfather hadn't been here to bail me out unless my mother didn't let them know I was locked up.

If I was going crazy and I hadn't even been locked up for twenty-four hours there was no way I could survive this for the rest of my life. I was ready to let the tears of defeat flow out but something inside me wouldn't let me do it. I was a fighter. I was born into a family of fighters and I couldn't let this break me. It wasn't too long ago I was in this same predicament—locked up. "If I got through it once I would get through it again", I said out loud thinking back to how the more things change the more they stay the same.

It had been a few weeks since Amir's birthday party and my mother and I were barely on speaking terms, which was fine by me. At this point I didn't want to ever speak to her. I hated her for cheating on my dad and I hated it even more that I couldn't say anything. Although Amir really turned me the fuck off by the stupid shit he said to me at the party I was a person of my word. I told him I wouldn't let the shit slip out about my mom and Lorenzo so that was a done deal but it made me full of resentment. My dad adored my mother and if he knew some other man had taken his place it would destroy him.

"Aaliyah, we need to talk." The sound of my mother's voice broke me out of the depressing place my mind was in.

"I can't right now. I'm meeting D'Mario and I'm already late."

"Then he won't mind waiting a little longer."

"He won't but I do."

"Aaliyah, I'm not going to tolerate your disrespect. I'm your mother."

"Then act like it. Because the mother I know or I thought I knew wouldn't be sneaking around having an affair with another man." My mother swallowed hard and I could see her cheeks turning beet red. Her hair was pulled tightly in a ponytail so there was no hiding what she felt, as every emotion was exposed on her face.

"I'm not going to discuss my relationship with

Lorenzo anymore with you. You asked me to consider my marriage and how it would affect Xavier and that's what I'm doing."

"Good, I hope you make the right decision, now excuse me I have to go."

"Wait," my mother said grabbing my arm as I was walking past her to exit the kitchen. "We need to discuss your relationship with D'Mario."

"What's there to discuss, he's my boyfriend."

"It's taking everything in me not to slap the shit out of you."

"Why? Because I'm being upfront and in the open about my relationship with D'Mario instead of creeping around like I'm starring in some disastrous Lifetime miniseries."

"That's enough, Aaliyah!"

"You're such a hypocrite. You judge D'Mario because he sells drugs but you're a married woman having an affair with a man that does the exact same thing."

"You don't know what you're talking about!"

"Yes I do. I'm not naïve, mother. I know what Genesis does, my dad, Lorenzo and my grandfather before he retired out the game. So don't stand there and judge D'Mario. You need to look long and hard at yourself."

POW!

That slap I knew was coming finally landed across my right cheek. It didn't shake me up because I knew my mother and if anything I was expecting it to come sooner.

"How dare you. Everything I am, everything I've

become is out of my love for you. I would walk to the end of this earth for you. I would battle, fight and kill for you. You and Xavier are my life. The reason I don't want you with D'Mario isn't because I'm trying to judge him. It's because I've been there and I've done it better than you'll ever be able to do it and one thing I know as fact, is that you can never beat the streets. If you stay too long and don't get out, the streets will beat you. I don't want that for you Aaliyah. I didn't almost die more times than you can count so my only daughter can end up catching the prison term or God forbid the death sentence that I always managed to escape."

"I hear you, but it won't happen to me. Now excuse me I have to go." I bolted out the kitchen before my mother had a chance to stop me. I was tired of listening to her and couldn't take anymore.

When I got in the car, I turned on the ignition, pressed down on the gas, speeding to D'Mario's place. If a cop stopped me and gave me a ticket I wouldn't have cared but it didn't happen. Why? Because I was one of the lucky ones, bad things didn't happen to me. For the last couple of months I had been meeting D'Mario's connect and picking up the envelope with no problems. Why? Because again, I'm one of the lucky ones. That's what I kept telling myself because believing that was a lot more fun than acknowledging that what my mother had said could end up being true.

What normally was a twenty minute ride to D'Mario's place, I got there in about ten. I rushed to the front door and unlocked it since he had given me a key. He had been so patient with me and paying generously for my simple pickup services, that I decided today I would reward him. I actually just made the decision after the heated confrontation with my mom. Everything I knew she would loathe, I wanted to do it and it would start with me losing my virginity to D'Mario today.

"Baby, I was starting to think you weren't coming," D'Mario said when I opened the door. He was lying on the couch with some sweats on and a wife beater that exposed his lean but muscular arms. The man owned sexy without even trying and I wondered how I was able to go so long without giving it up, but that was about to change.

Without saying a word I mounted myself on top of D'Mario, letting our tongues interlock promptly. His hands massaged my hardened nipples as I felt his dick growing under me. "Baby, let's not do this. I don't feel like jackin' my shit off."

"You don't have to."

D'Mario gently pushed me away, and asked, "What did you say?"

"You don't have to because you can cum while we're making love. Then we'll stop and start all over again."

"Are you telling me you're ready?"

"Yes."

"But after making me wait so long I wanted to take you to Anguilla or somewhere like that and we have sex on the beach...something romantic."

"So are you turning me down and saying you want to wait?" I gave him a devilish grin.

"Hell No! You might change your mind and I've

wanted you so bad since the first time I saw you going into the mall. If you're going to give yourself to me now then I'll take you now."

"I am ready." I lifted up the gray t-shirt dress I was wearing over my head and D'Mario wasted no time unclipping my bra. He cupped my breasts and his soft wet lips began going back and forth getting a mouthful of my nipples each time. I moaned out in pleasure anticipating how amazing he would feel, filling up my insides. "Take off your shirt," I whispered wanting to see his ripped abs.

He obliged by not only taking off his shirt but his sweat pants too. When he stood up it was the first time I had ever seen him completely naked and the man was built like a fuckin' black stallion.

"Damn you fine," he said to me when I stood up and slid out my panties. "Let me take you upstairs so we can make love in the bed."

"We can make love here first and then you can take me upstairs to your bed...I'm in no rush." D'Mario smiled at me with those beautiful dimples and pretty white teeth. He laid me down on the couch and spread my legs so his tongue could deflower me first. As I closed my eyes eagerly anticipating this mind blowing experience I heard so much about, somehow in less than sixty seconds with what sounded like an explosion, I went from a dream world to a complete nightmare.

"Stand up and put your hands behind your head! D'Mario Faine and Aaliyah Mills Carter you're under arrest for conspiracy to possess with the intent to distribute cocaine, using the telephone to facilitate a drug crime and..." I couldn't hear anything after that. If it wasn't for the fact that my tits were jiggling and my ass was exposed in front of a ton of federal agents I would never have believed this was happening to me. I was speechless. I wasn't even able to put the simple words together like cover me the fuck up. I was screaming it in my head but it was like when I opened my mouth there was nothing. Therefore I continued to keep my eyes closed, praying that when I opened them the nightmare would be over.

After being photographed, fingerprinted, given a brief examination by the jail nurse, then issued a jumpsuit with some slip on shoes and thrown into a jail cell, I had to face reality that this nightmare wasn't going away. I hadn't even called my parents or anybody because I didn't know what to say because I was still confused by what happened. So when the guard told me I was being released I didn't know what to think but he didn't have to tell me twice.

I couldn't rip that jumpsuit off fast enough. I put my street clothes back on and was lead to the front but when I got there I wanted to go right back to where I came from. My mother and father were waiting for me and I had never seen either one of them look as angry as they were at that very moment. I literally wouldn't take another step forward. The officer had to grab my wrist and move me along.

"Don't say a word until we get in the car," was the welcoming my dad gave me. My mother simply murdered me twice with the way she slit her eyes at me. As I retrieved my belongings and we were walking out the last person any of us needed to see came in.

"What are you doing, stalking us?" my mother shouted.

"Calm down, Precious. This isn't the place or time for a scene."

"My dear sister, why would I want to stalk you?" Maya asked in a condescending tone. "Your life is pretty boring, or at least it was until your daughter decided to follow in her *real* father's footsteps."

"Maya, I am not your sister."

"According to a DNA match you are but that's irrelevant. I'm not here to see you."

"So it's strictly a coincidence that you showed up at the same jail at the same time as me."

"That would be correct. If you must know, I'm here on behalf of my man Darius, who happens to be the brother of my niece's boyfriend. Isn't this a small world?"

"Darius is your boyfriend! And you've known all this time that I'm seeing his brother? What type of sick game are you playing, Maya."

"Aaliyah, don't say another word," my dad warned.

"Look at you, Supreme, still playing that protective daddy role, for a child that's not even yours." My dad flinched forward and my mom quickly moved in front of him.

"She's not worth it, Supreme," my mom said being the voice of reason. "Come on, Aaliyah, let's go." I followed behind my parents and then lingered back so I could confront Maya.

I marched right up to her and used a soft tone but let my words speak loud and clear. "If I find out that you had anything to do with D'Mario's or my arrest I promise you, what my mother didn't have the heart to finish I will."

"Should they add terroristic threat to the long list of charges you're already facing? One additional charge won't make a dent in those twenty years you're about to be facing."

"Fuck you, Maya. Just remember what I said and..." Right when I was attempting to finish letting Maya know what was up my mom came back in to get me.

"Aaliyah, get over here now!" Then my mother sauntered over to Maya pointing her long slender finger in her face. "Stay away from my daughter. If you see her coming, go the opposite way. If I even hear that you accidentally ran into her you will experience a blackout. And don't even bother asking me if that was a threat because we both know, I don't make threats I deliver on promises. So we're clear that right there was a promise."

My mother grabbed my arm and I rolled my eyes at Maya as we made our exit. I truly wanted to take my foot and stomp the life out of Maya. She was always plotting and lurking waiting for the right moment to show her evil face. I didn't know to what degree but I would bet my life that she had something to do with what happened to me and D'Mario. During the entire car ride home all I was trying to figure out was what role did she play? Because both my mother and father weren't saying a word to me or each other it gave me plenty of time to come up with some scenarios but I kept drawing a blank.

When we arrived home I saw my grandfather's car parked in the driveway. I silently thanked God because I was hoping his presence would save me from the wrath of my mother. The fact she hadn't said a word to me since we got in the car let me know that a volcano would erupt once we got in the house. I took my time getting out the car and going into the house as if it would make a difference on how harsh of a tongue lashing I was set to get.

Somehow no matter how slow I was, we all ended up arriving in the living room at the same time. It was like my parents had slowed their pace so I could keep up with them, which is what I didn't want. "Grandfather, I'm so happy to see you." I practically jumped into his arms like I was four years old instead of eighteen.

"How are you?" even with an arrest under my belt my grandfather spoke to me in the same endearing, loving voice he always did.

"Better, now that you're here." My grandfather gently rubbed my back like he always did when he thought I seemed stressed.

"Stop babying her. That's why she's a spoiled brat now," my mother snapped, making me hold on even tighter to my grandfather. I knew shit was about to explode but I was hoping for a longer reprieve.

"I'm not babying her, Precious. She's had a traumatic night."

"She brought it on herself. I warned you to stay away from that man but you refused to listen. Now look at you, facing drug charges! You're going to have an arrest record what type of future is that!"

"Aaliyah, your mother is right. Is this guy the same person you introduced me to at Amir's birthday party?"

"Yes."

"He seemed like a good guy. Did you know he was a drug dealer before you were arrested today?"

"Supreme, don't be naïve. Of course she knew! But like always, Aaliyah wants to do what she wants to do."

"I guess that's another trait we share in common, mother."

"I'ma slap the shit outta you," my mother barked lunging towards me. My father grabbed her arm holding her back.

"Precious, calm down. This is not some street fight you're in. This is our daughter. And, Aaliyah, don't speak to your mother like that."

"Daddy, she's not worth defending. If you only kn..." my mother cut me off with such swiftness by the roar of her voice I thought I went deaf.

"Aaliyah, that's enough! This is about you and the poor decisions you choose to make!" There was so much I wanted to scream right back at my mother but I held my tongue. This wasn't the right time. My family was already in the middle of a storm and I didn't need to make it worse.

"All of you calm down and listen to what I have to say." My grandfather demanded. "Aaliyah was released because a very close friend of mine who is high up in the ranks with the Feds informed me about the arrest. He didn't know you were my granddaughter until after the fact. But all the charges against Aaliyah will be dropped."

"Thank you, Jesus," my father shouted, sitting down on the sofa folding his hands as if praying to God.

"Quentin, I don't know how to thank you. You always manage to come up with a miracle. This time I'm happy it wasn't for Maya but instead for my daughter."

"It wasn't that difficult. The only concrete evidence they had on Aaliyah was her going to meet a connect and picking up an envelope a few times."

"That sonofabitch had you working for him!" My mother went right back to attack mode.

"No. I asked him to let me do it. I didn't think it was a big deal. I was wrong and I made a mistake. Can we let it go? Grandfather said the charges will be dropped against me. That's all that matters."

"I hope you've learned your lesson from this because one day your grandfather might not be able to get you out of one of your fucked up predicaments." I ignored what my mother said because I had other things on my mind like what was going to happen to D"Mario.

"Grandfather, what about D'Mario. Are the charges going to be dropped against him?"

"Why do you even care? He was using you! Having you do his dirty work."

"That's not true. Our relationship wasn't like that at all."

"Aaliyah, there is nothing that can be done for D'Mario. They've been watching him and his brother for a long time, trying to build a case. I didn't know that. If I had I would've warned Maya to make a clean break from Darius. So D'Mario won't be getting out of jail for a very long time."

"So you knew about Maya and Darius?"

"Yes, that's how I knew when I saw you with D'Mario that he was a drug dealer and not eighteen. Maya has been seeing his brother for some time now."

"Did you tell Maya about me and D'Mario?"

"No. I was under the impression that you had severed all ties with him after the conversation me and your mother had with you in the kitchen. I had no idea the two of you were still involved until after your arrest today."

"Grandfather, Maya came to the police station when we were leaving and I'm telling you she had something to do with it."

"Do with what?"

"Our arrest."

"I told you the Feds have been watching both brothers and their operation for a while now."

"Then why wasn't Darius arrested?"

"You never know why the Feds do what they do but I'm sure they are working on it."

"Enough about Maya and those damn brothers. Let's rejoice in the fact that those charges will be dropped against you and we can put this craziness behind us."

"I agree with your mother and thank you, Quentin. I don't care how you managed to do it, you saved my daughter and I'll always be grateful to you for that."

"Supreme, you know I would do anything for this family."

"You've proven that again and again, I thank you. Now Aaliyah," my dad turned his attention toward me. "You have to make better choices. You're eighteen. Although you'll always be my little girl to the world you're a grownup and second chances are rarely given."

"You're right, daddy. And I'm sorry. I have to be more responsible with my decisions and I will be."

"Good, now give me a hug."

"It's been a long night so I'm going to let you all get some rest," my grandfather said. "I'll talk to you tomorrow."

"I'll walk you out," my father said, patting my grandfather on the shoulder.

"Thanks again, Quentin." My mother gave her dad a hug goodbye, something I had never witnessed before.

"My pleasure," he said taking great pride in being able to hug his daughter back, seeing that exchange touched me. With all the negativity I went through today it was such a relief for it to end on a positive note. I decided to head upstairs to take a hot shower and wash off the last reminder of what happened.

"Aaliyah, wait," I heard my mother say. I wanted to keep going upstairs but I knew if I didn't stop to hear what she had to say she would simply follow me to my room.

"Yes, mother," I replied in a peaceful voice, letting her know I wanted to call a truce.

"I didn't appreciate what you were about to say to your father but I'm glad you held it together and changed your mind."

"I didn't do it for you. I did it for daddy."

"Whatever the reason, you made the right decision."

"Only time will tell. Goodnight, mother."

I didn't know if the decision to keep my mother's affair from my dad was right or wrong but it was the choice I made and I would stick with it for now. If I learned one thing today it was that when you make a decision you have no control over the outcome so be prepared to deal with whatever ramifications that comes with it.

Amir

Words I Never Said

It seemed like Nico and my dad had been inside of the police station for hours but when I looked at my watch it had been nowhere close to that long. It was my nerves getting the best of me. With the craziness I went through today the one thing I did know was when I talked to Aaliyah again, I promised myself I would no longer hold back. I would tell her the truth and stop wasting time because it was too valuable. I thought about how much time I had already wasted. It seemed just the other day the three of us were making plans for how we would spend our summer vacation before starting college and now that break was almost over.

    "I'm so happy there is no more high school! We're going to have an awesome summer partying in New York and hanging out at my dad's crib in Jersey. I love being at his place. I always feel like I'm home alone when I stay here. He lives on a fuckin' estate and it's just him. We can be here for the entire summer and never see him if we wanted to."

"I know right! Thank goodness my mom and dad let me come with you. I wouldn't want to be anyplace else but lounging in this Jacuzzi with you guys, " Justina, said kissing the side of my neck.

"And to think with everything that went on with me a few months ago, I thought the only place you all would be visiting me at was behind a jail cell."

"Aaliyah, I'm not gonna lie, I'm glad you told me what happened after you were in the clear because I would've been stressing nonstop. But at the same time when it comes to your family I realize they can make a miracle out of the worse situations."

"Between Quentin, Supreme, Nico and my father there aren't too many problems that can't go away. You know I'm right."

"Of course, Amir, you're *always* right. Isn't he *always* right Justina?" Aaliyah mockingly put up her fingers doing quotations marks while stressing the word always. She and Justina both laughed and I couldn't help but join in.

"Hey, you have to admit, most of the times I am right. I don't have a problem with that and neither should the two of you."

"Baby, you know I love you being right all the time," Justina said giving me a kiss on the lips. I had to take it further and get some open mouth going.

"I didn't get on a plane and come all this way to watch the two of you tongue each other down," Aaliyah complained as I caught her rolling her eyes.

"I can't help it, I missed my, baby."

"I missed you too," I said kissing Justina on the tip of her nose.

"I guess since you all are still a couple this is what I have to look forward to the entire summer."

"That's why you need to get a boyfriend, Aaliyah, so you won't feel like a third wheel. Oh, and let me add, one that isn't going to have you end up in jail again."

"Funny, Justina. But honestly, I miss D'Mario. He was a great boyfriend. Do you know the day we got arrested we were actually about to have sex for the first time."

"Excuse me! When you told the story you conveniently left that part of it out."

"I was still dealing with the humiliation of getting arrested while I was fuckin' naked."

"Ha, ha, ha, ha, ha. I'm sorry, Aaliyah, I know I shouldn't be laughing but that's the funniest shit I've heard in a minute."

"I'm glad you think so, Justina."

"So you and D'Mario never had a chance to go all the way?"

"No. The Feds kicked the door in before we had an opportunity."

"So you're still a virgin, Aaliyah, Justina said shaking her head. "This is ridiculous. We have to find you a boyfriend. It's not fair that out of the two of us I'm the only one who has experienced how amazing sex is."

"Thanks for the reminder."

I was taken aback by Aaliyah's confession. I

thought for sure that night at my birthday party she had sex with D'Mario. I had no idea she was still a virgin. Her admission seemed to reopen all these feelings I had buried in a matter of seconds.

"Don't worry, I got you. You're my best friend and I guarantee you, before this summer is over you'll no longer be a virgin."

"Wow, Justina, that's a pretty huge guarantee."

"You'll see.

"Truth be told I hope you're right because I need to get over D'Mario."

"Have you talked to him?"

"A few times and I even went to visit him and my parents flipped out."

"I can imagine. The charges were dropped against you. The last thing you need to be doing is communicating with him. I'm sure they're recording your conversations anyway."

"I'm not saying anything to incriminate myself I'm not that stupid."

"But Justina's right, it really is in your best interest to cut off all communication."

"I know. That's why I went to go see him. I wanted to tell him in person that I cared about him but he couldn't call me anymore."

"I bet he didn't take that very well."

"He took it a lot better than I thought he would. He understood and agreed that was the best thing for me to do. He knows he's not getting out anytime soon and he told me it was time for me to move on with my life."

"Wow, that was big of him."

"I know. D'Mario really is a great guy. I wish him the best but I have college and the summer to look forward to and that's what I'm going to focus on."

"That's a great idea, don't you think, Amir...Amir, where is your head at right now?" Justina asked nudging my arm. I didn't think it was a good idea to inform her that my top head was thinking how relieved I was that Aaliyah hadn't lost her virginity to D'Mario and my bottom head was wishing I could be her first.

"I was just wondering what we should do tonight."

"I'm glad you brought that up because that's the surprise I wanted to share with you guys."

"What surprise?"

"My dad got us tickets to Sway Stone's concert tonight at Madison Square Garden."

"Get out! With everything that's been going on I totally forgot about his concert. Remember, Amir, I told you about it months ago!"

"He's one of my dad's clients under his advertising and marketing services company. So we have an all access pass to everything!"

"You're shittin' me!"

"Nope!"

"T-Roc Rocks! I should talk to my dad about partnering with your dad just so I can get me some Sway Stone perks. But then my dad isn't that cool with your dad because of my other dad, so that isn't going to work."

"It could. My dad is really close to Genesis not so much to Nico. They're cool because Genesis and Nico are business partners. But I think it would be awesome if your dad and my dad partnered up."

"I think that's just wishful thinking on our part. As long as we've been friends if they haven't done it by now then it ain't gonna happen. But who cares as long as somebody has the Sway Stone hookup."

"Baby, why are you so quiet? I thought you would be more excited than Aaliyah."

"I'm kinda over the whole Sway Stone thing."

"Since when? You love his music."

"It's a'ight."

"Anyway, everything is set. We even have backstage passes so we can meet Sway before the show."

"I'ma have to pass and I think you all should too."

"Why would we want to do that?"

"I heard some things about him, that's all."

"Things like what?"

"For one that he does drugs."

"From what my dad told me, just about everybody in that business does drugs. As long as we're not snorting coke and poppin' pills who cares."

"I should've expected that answer from you, Aaliyah."

"And what is that supposed to mean, Amir? I mean when did you become so self-righteous. Considering some of the history of our parents, I don't think any of us has room to judge others...ya think!"

"I'm not being self-righteous or judging. People aren't the way you think sometimes, that's all I'm saying."

"Baby, please come tonight. It won't be the same without you," Justina smiled while rubbing the back of my neck."

"She's right, Amir. It wouldn't be the same without you. I want you with us."

"Fine, I'll go," I said not wanting to get into a long drawn out debate with them. I didn't want to take the chance of slipping up. As close as the three of us were I couldn't tell them that my dad was helping Lorenzo plot on that man's life. That was business and my dad always stressed the importance of being able to separate friendship and business when needed. My dad had chosen to help out Lorenzo because they were friends and they also did business together. I couldn't risk jeopardizing their relationship because I got caught shooting off at the mouth to Aaliyah and Justina. Having my dad's respect meant more to me than anything and I wasn't going to disappoint him. I would have to keep my feelings about Sway to myself plain and simple.

When we arrived at Madison Square Garden the show had already started. I wanted to catch the end of the opening act but all Aaliyah and Justina wanted to do was get backstage.

"Come on, Amir. We're already late. I hope the guy my dad had meeting us hasn't left."

"Don't rush me. You and Aaliyah were the ones taking a year and a day to get ready for this clown."

"What is up with you? You were the biggest Sway fan, now you act like you're allergic to the dude. I hope you're not jealous because my only interest is in you."

I stopped walking for a second and stared at

Justina. I was making sure I heard her right. "You really think I'm jealous of that dude?"

"Will you two come on," I heard Aaliyah scream out, as she was way ahead of us.

"Amir, we can talk about this later. Let's just enjoy our night and have fun."

"Whatever," I said nonchalantly and continued to walk forward.

When we made it to the open entrance, it was blocked off and mad security was obstructing any sort of entrance. It was a bunch of people hollering that they had passes to get backstage but nobody was producing shit.

"So where is the man that your dad said would hook us up. 'Cause I'm not about to be standing here looking crazy like the rest of those fools," Aaliyah said as she cut her eyes towards the crowd in front of us.

"You all took so long to get dressed and get down here, that man probably bounced by now."

"Stop being so negative, Amir."

"I'm not being negative, I'm being real. I'm sure that man has other things to do besides wait around for us." At least that was what I was hoping. I could tolerate watching the concert from our seats but I didn't want to be backstage with Sway and his entourage. Right when it looked like all my hoping would pay off I noticed this super skinny tall guy in a suit approaching us.

"Hi, aren't you Justina, T-Roc's daughter?"

"Yes!"

"I'm Robert. I've been looking for you."

"We're a little late. I was worried you left us."

"Your dad gave me strict instructions to wait for you because he said you would definitely be showing up."

"He was right about that."

"So how many people do you have with you?"

"It's just three of us."

"Great. I thought at least half of the girls standing in that line over there were with you."

"No, we don't roll like that. It's just three of us in our clique," Aaliyah stated, stepping up on Robert.

"Robert, that's my friend Aaliyah. And this is my boyfriend Amir."

"Nice to meet you both," he said acknowledging us both with a handshake. "We better get going. Backstage with Sway can get a little out of hand."

When we entered Sway's dressing room I was expecting something the size of a huge oversized closet but instead it looked like the size of a humongous apartment. People were scattered in different sections of the room, talking, eating and drinking. I was scanning the room to see if I could spot Sway but instead I noticed my Aunt Nichelle.

"Where are you going?" I heard Justina call out as I made my way across the room.

"I'll be right back," I said putting my finger up. I was positive that Justina wouldn't mind since the only thing that seemed to be on her mind was meeting Sway Stone.

My Aunt was so deep in conversation she didn't even notice I was walking up on her until I said her name. "Aunt Nichelle, what are you doing here?"

"I need to be asking you that question," she smiled giving me a hug.

"Justina's dad got us tickets and the backstage hookup. Now your turn."

"One of the girls I'm representing is working tonight."

"I thought you represented models not singers."

"I do. Sway is doing this series of commercials and they wanted it to have a day in the real life feel, like a documentary. Part of that is filming him before he takes the stage at the legendary Madison Square Garden. And the young lady I represent is one of the main girls in the commercial. I'm here making sure all goes well."

"So you're here protecting your investment."

"You're sounding more and more like my brother every day."

"That's a good thing. My dad is always about business. Did you mention to him you're working with Sway Stone."

"Yes. As a matter of fact, the young lady in the commercial is a model that one of his business partners introduced me to."

"You must be talking about Lorenzo."

"Yeah, that is his name."

"I was on my way to curse you out for leaving me and coming to flirt with some chick and then I realized it was Nichelle...hey Nichelle," Justina said interrupting my conversation with my aunt.

"Hey, Justina! It's good to see you oh and here comes Aaliyah. The whole gang is in attendance."

"What's up Nichelle!"

"Hi, Aaliyah! You look beautiful as always."

"So do you. Let me find out you attending backstage parties. That fine husband of yours doesn't have a problem with that," Aaliyah said nudging Nichelle's arm in a joking way.

"Renny understands the business I'm in and I'm here working."

"Whatever you want to call it. We all got to hustle and I'm not knocking yours. But do tell, did you get invited here after doing some sort of modeling gig for Sway Stone?"

"Aaliyah, I stopped modeling a couple years ago. I have my own agency now."

"I told you that, Aaliyah. Remember the article I showed you they did on her a few months ago in that magazine."

"Amir, we talk about so much stuff but I don't recall that. But congrats, Nichelle, on your agency. Why did you give up modeling though? You still got it!"

"Honestly, I got fed up with having a career where everything relied on my looks. I'll leave that to the new girls on the come up. But at least because I've experienced mostly everything they're going through I can help lead them in the right direction."

"So is one of your girls working here tonight?"

"Yep, and here she comes now."

"If we had to do that take one more time I was going to scream."

"That's part of the business. Everybody this is Courtney. Courtney, this is my nephew Amir, his girlfriend Justina and best friend Aaliyah." I took a good look at the girl Courtney and like I expected she was the young lady I saw at my birthday party who was in that intense conversation with my dad, aunt and Lorenzo. She had to be the woman Lorenzo had told my dad would be perfect to infiltrate Sway's circle, all she needed was a legitimate introduction which they clearly found with my Aunt Nichelle's help.

"It's good to meet you guys. Are you looking forward to the show?"

"Definitely!" Aaliyah and Justina said at the same time.

"What about you?"

"I'm sure it will be cool."

"Speaking of cool, look who's coming!" Justina said elbowing my arm. "And where did Aaliyah disappear to that quick? She's going to miss her opportunity to meet Sway."

I noticed Aaliyah a few feet away over at the bar area getting a drink while making small talk with some guy. Before I could tell Justina, she was all up in Sway's grill practically drooling. I knew she was a huge fan but I had never seen her act so thirsty over a guy before. I let her continue acting like a borderline groupie and went to get Aaliyah. I figured she would want to get in on the act too.

"I hate to interrupt but I thought you would want to know that Sway is right over there," I said nodding my head in his direction. "Aaliyah, did you hear what I said?" I questioned because instead of hauling ass in Sway's path, she started getting extra flirtatious with the random dude she was talking to at the bar. "Aaliyah, are you coming or what? I'm sure Sway is about to go on stage any minute. This is gonna be your only opportunity to meet him."

"Amir, can't you see I'm busy. Sway can wait." Aaliyah went back to laughing, smiling seductively and rubbing on the random dude's face. I was confused but before I could start tripping Sway and his bodyguard had walked up on us.

"I know you saw me looking at you. What's your name?" I knew he couldn't be talking to me and there wasn't any other female around besides Aaliyah so he had to be talking to her. But she kept laughing as if she didn't even notice that there was a superstar rapper standing in front of her face asking her a question. "So you're just going to ignore me?" he asked as if stunned.

"I apologize, were you speaking to me?" Aaliyah inquired so damn casually that you would've actually believed she didn't know.

"Yeah, I was. What's your name?"

"Aaliyah."

"How old are you?"

"Eighteen."

"That's good, you're legal."

"Yeah, I'm legal. And of course there is no need for you to introduce yourself. You're Sway Stone. I love your music and so does my friend Amir," Aaliyah said, pointing at me.

"What's up," I said but Sway didn't even look in my direction.

"Glad you're a fan. I'm having a private party after my show. I want you to be my guest."

"That's so sweet but I can't." Aaliyah put her head down like she was on some bashful bullshit.

"What do you mean you can't?" Sway asked as if he hadn't heard that word before.

"I have an early flight to catch back to LA tomorrow and I haven't even packed yet. So thanks for the invite but I have to pass."

I couldn't believe the bullshit coming out of Aaliyah's mouth. I didn't know what she was trying to do but whatever it was it seemed to be frustrating the fuck out of Sway and I was loving that shit.

"You have to pass," Sway repeated as if him saying it out loud would make Aaliyah change her answer.

"Yeah, I do."

"So what do you do, Aaliyah?"

"I'm in school."

"So you're on summer break?"

"Yes, why?"

"Just trying to figure out your availability."

"My availability?"

"Yes. I'll be in touch," Sway said and walked away.

"What was that about?" I asked Aaliyah as she turned her head and burst out laughing.

"Yo, I played that shit so cool."

"Yeah, maybe a little too cool."

"Please, you heard him. He said he would be in touch."

"That was him just trying to act like it was all good because you turned him down. He won't be in touch. His ego won't let him."

"Amir, you have no idea how this game works."

"Excuse me. Since you know, explain it to me."

"First of all, it's because of his ego that Sway will be in touch. You know how long it's been since somebody turned him down."

"Is that why you did it?"

"Of course! My mother always told me, treat the man you want like you don't want him in order to get him."

"What?"

"It's called playing hard to get. It's the oldest but still most reliable rule in the player's handbook."

"If you say so, but I believe you've missed your opportunity to score with Sway Stone and I'm glad. He's not what you need anyway." Right when I was about to break down all the reasons, Justina popped up.

"Look, I got Sway's autograph and he took a picture with me. He's so sweet. I saw you guys over here talking to him. What did he say?"

"Nothing really, he invited Aaliyah to be his guest at the after party." I watched Justina's eyes widen and her mouth drop.

"We're partying with Sway after the concert tonight. I can't believe this," Justina smiled.

"I left out the part where Aaliyah turned him down. She told him she had a flight to catch to LA in the morning."

"What! We're not going back to LA, we just got here."

"We know that but Aaliyah wanted to play hard to get."

"You're playing hard to get with Sway Stone, are you crazy! How can you miss out on a once in a lifetime opportunity like that?"

"Justina, it's not that serious. I'll have another chance with Sway, trust me."

"What if you don't!" Justina barked.

"Yo, calm yo' ass down. I do think Aaliyah took her hard to get game too far but I rather her play that role than that of a groupie."

"I ain't acting like no groupie!"

"First, you all up in dude's grill acting thirsty now you coming down on Aaliyah because she played coy. I mean let her do her. "

"Whatever Amir, you've been acting salty about Sway since you found out I had tickets to the concert. Don't call me a groupie because you're jealous."

"Would the two of you stop! I mean this shit is getting real petty. Let's just go watch the concert and have fun."

I couldn't believe Aaliyah was being the voice of reason. Normally Justina or I would have to calm her ass down but this time we seemed out of control. I suppose Justina was right; there was some jealousy on my part but not over her, instead it came from watching Sway step to Aaliyah. It did piss me off watching my girlfriend act all extra over some other nigga especially since I didn't expect that from her. Justina always seemed so reserved and safe. That was the main reason I chose her over Aaliyah. My dad constantly reminded me never get serious with a woman that's a headache because life will bring you enough of those without a woman adding to it. I thought Aaliyah, not Justina would be my headache but maybe I was wrong.

Aaliyah

Hell Of A Life

"Your attorney hasn't arrived yet but I thought you would want to know your father is here," the police officer informed me.

"Can I see him?"

"No."

"What was the point of you telling me that if you weren't going to let me see him, asshole," I screamed out while he was walking away. It was like he was purposely fucking with me. But it was nice to know that somebody was finally here on my behalf. At first I was going to ask which dad but I knew it had to be Nico since he mentioned nothing about my mother. I wondered what was taking her and my dad so long to get here. We hadn't been on the best of terms lately but she was my mother and she wouldn't abandon ship on me or would she? I couldn't pinpoint if my concern was coming from a real place or was it because I was fucking exhausted.

My head was spinning. I didn't understand how I began my summer feeling on top of the world but now I was seriously debating if my mother had any intentions of coming to see if she could bail me out of jail. As I began to doze off I thought about how positive things had been recently and I would give anything to get that time back.

"That concert was awesome last night," I commented to Justina as we sat outside by the pool drinking Bellini's.

"Awesome is not a big enough word to describe what we experienced last night. It's one thing to listen to Sway Stone's music on a CD and entirely different thing hearing him live in concert."

"You get no argument from me."

"And to only think, we could've partied with him personally if you hadn't fucked it up."

"I didn't fuck anything up."

"We're here, and there's no Sway Stone. I call that a fuck up."

"Call it whatever you like," I said before answering my phone. "Hello."

"Hey, Aaliyah, did I catch you at a bad time?"

"Umm, who is this?"

"Sorry, about that. It's me Nichelle. Amir gave me your number."

"Hi, Nichelle. I didn't recognize your voice. What's going on?"

"That's what I'm calling to find out from you."

"Really." I eyed Justina letting her know that I was completely perplexed by this phone call from Nichelle.

"What does she want?" I hit the mute button so Nichelle couldn't hear my response.

"I'm trying to figure that out," I said then hit the mute button again so I could wrap this phone call up with Nichelle and get back to drinking my Bellini. "Well, I'm at my dad's house relaxing by the pool with Justina. Did you want to join us or something?"

I extended the invite because I didn't understand what the hell she was calling me for and I didn't know what else to say. Nichelle no doubt seemed like a cool chick but I all I really knew about her was she used to be a model, had a fine ass husband named Renny and she had a little boy. It was really her husband's son that he had with her dead best friend but she was raising him like he was her own. I think I had the story right but Amir told me what sounded like a soap opera street tale so long ago I might have it wrong, The point was I really didn't know what she would want to talk to me about.

"That's sweet of you to ask, maybe another time."

"No problem. But I'm about to take a dip in the pool so I'll call you back later, Nichelle."

"Aaliyah wait!" She yelled out as I was about to end the call.

"Yes, Nichelle." I was trying to keep my patience because this was Amir's aunt and I did remember her babysitting us a couple times when we were little, although she didn't seem to be too much older than us. But this phone call was starting to make me think she had some weirdo tendencies.

"I was calling because I wanted to see if you were interested in doing some modeling this summer before you started school."

"Gosh, Nichelle, why didn't you just say that when you first called. I was starting to think you were strange."

"No need to think that. So are you interested?"

"It depends. Do I have to go audition or do you already have something lined up?"

"I have something already on the table for you." I wasn't expecting that answer from Nichelle. I figured she would tell me about a few potential gigs that I would have to interview for and I was going to then politely decline. I had no desire to spend my entire summer on the east coast going on one 'go see' after another and being turned down. I had better things to do like shop, drink, party and flirt with cute boys. So since she had something already lined up I assumed it wasn't paying and again I would decline. Yes, I was technically a trust fund baby with access to plenty of money but I wasn't doing shit for free.

"So what you have on the table is it paying?" I made a bubble with my gum waiting for Nichelle to drop the magic deal killer word, 'no'.

"Definitely! I would never offer you a gig that wasn't paying. If there's no money being made it's not a job it's a hobby."

"So what gig is it?" I was curious to know now that Nichelle had my full attention.

"Sway Stone wants you to replace one of the models for the series of commercials he's doing."

"Really, and when would I start?"

"Immediately. So I would need your answer now."

"Yes, I'll do it."

"Great! I'll have a car pick you up from your dad's house in an hour. Can you be ready?"

"Definitely." When I hung up with Nichelle, I couldn't stop laughing.

"What is so funny? What did Nichelle say?"

"Guess who personally requested me to replace one of the models in the series of commercial he's doing."

"Don't fuckin' play with me right now."

"You ruined your opportunity with Sway Stone," I whined in an annoying voice mimicking Justina.

"You're gonna be in a commercial with Sway Stone! You lucky bitch! I so hate you right now!"

"Don't hate...appreciate," I started clapping, singing and playing with the words turning it into a little song.

"So when do you start?"

"Nichelle will have a car here to pick me up in an hour. So this lucky bitch needs to get up and get ready."

"Can I come with you?"

"I don't think it would be a good idea for you to come with me on my first official day at work. But let me vibe everything out and see if I can bring you from now on. Maybe I can tell them you're my personal assistant."

"It didn't take you long to turn into a diva."

"I was trying to find a way to fit you in. But fine, you can figure out what's going on by the pics I send you through my phone. Talk to you later."

When I arrived to the closed set in Time Square

where they were about to film a scene for the commercial, everything seemed to be in full swing. There were a couple models, including the girl I saw at the concert last night getting their makeup touched up, I noticed a group of dancers practicing their choreography and then there was a large entourage and I assumed that was Sway and his people.

"Aaliyah, you made it," Nichelle said excitedly, greeting me with a hug. "Follow me, hair, makeup and wardrobe awaits you." Before I even had time to think or ask a question there were three different people working on me.

"This is a bit much," I grumbled.

"I know. But with everything happening so fast with you being a last minute replacement we're tight on time."

"I get that."

"I know with all the hoopla going on it won't be easy to do but try to relax and enjoy the moment," Nichelle suggested. "I have to go check on some other things but I'll be back."

"Take your time." I was hoping she never came back, I didn't need a babysitter. As I sat in the chair all I kept saying to myself was damn these motherfuckers fast. They were transforming me into a model within a matter of minutes. While relishing in my supermodel treatment I realized that Sway hadn't said anything to me since I arrived. I found it odd since the only reason I was here was because of him.

"Here, put this on and you're all set," a bubbly blonde said handing me an itty bitty bikini. I was all for showing off some skin but these pieces of thread she handed me was intimidatingly tiny. I took a deep breath, headed to the dressing room and put it on. When I came out, they had me put on some nude leather peep-toe, silver-tone stud embellishment Louboutin, add a collar pendant necklace with a rhinestone spike stretch bracelet. The jewelry and shoes turned the stripper bikini to a stylish ensemble. I was impressed.

"Aaliyah, I'm speechless. You were always a beautiful girl but you look simply breathtaking," Nichelle said shaking her head in astonishment.

As I looked at myself in the mirror I had to admit that makeup chick beat my face like I stole her man. My hair and everything was nothing less than perfection. A bitch was flawless and I loved every minute of it.

"Yeah, everybody did a great job."

"True, but if you didn't have that face and body to work with I don't care how great they are, they couldn't have created this."

"You do have a point," I laughed.

"Now come on, they're waiting for you."

When I came out everyone was in their allotted position and they all stared at me like where the hell is this bitch supposed to go. I followed Nichelle and she stuck me next to the model I saw yesterday and some Asian chick which was fine with me. I was looking hot, that's all I cared about.

"Okay, everybody get ready, we're about to start," the set director announced and I simply duplicated what the other two models were doing.

"Wait."

"Yes, Sway," the director said as if he was used to Sway interrupting him.

"I want her next to me," he said pointing to me. Everybody stared in my direction like who, what and where did she come from, especially the model that was already standing right next to Sway.

"Are you sure that's what you want, Sway?"

"Positive."

"Okay, you two switch places."

"What are you talking about?" the model stood there with her arms folded like she was puzzled by the switch.

"You go over there," the director clarified by moving both arms in my direction, "and she's coming over here," he then moved his arms back to the position she was standing in.

"But I'm a real supermodel. I'm supposed to be in the front."

"I'm the only super anything here," Sway stressed incase the model had any misconceptions. "This is my commercial. So either take yo' bony ass over there or get the fuck off the set. It's your call but make it quick because we need to keep this moving." The girl came over with the most mortified expression on her face. I didn't need him to explain it to me. I went and took my position.

"I see you missed your flight to LA."

"You got jokes," I smirked.

"We're going to have a lot of fun together, Aaliyah. And by the way, you look fuckin' incredible."

"You mean that don't you."

"Damn right, or you wouldn't be standing next to me. You're going to be mine and you'll enjoy every second of it."

"What if I don't want to be yours?"

"That's not even a possibility. Now stand there and make the world fall in love with you, that's what you're getting paid for."

I moved my body, posing trying to emulate what the other models were doing but only better. I didn't know what I had gotten myself into by willingly becoming a participant in this game with Sway. It was exciting and scary at the same time. So I did what any eighteen year old would do, sat back and got ready to enjoy the ride.

For the next few weeks I stayed up under Sway. He wouldn't let me move without him and because I was getting paid handsomely he didn't get an argument from me. But we both knew it went beyond money, I was falling fast for him. Or maybe I was falling for his fast paced superstar lifestyle. It didn't make a difference it was all intoxicating. From the parties, traveling and simply being in his presence, Sway was the personification of the overindulgent icon.

"Tomorrow is the last day of shooting for the commercials."

"I know, Nichelle told me."

"But I want to keep you with me. What do I need to do to make sure that happens?"

"I don't want to go anywhere. I like being with you."

"I know but I like to keep things that I have developed an attachment for under contract."

"That's different."

"I'm different. So how much does it cost for me to keep you under contract?"

"I'm puzzled by why you want me so bad."

"Because you remind me of my last girlfriend," he said caressing the side of my cheek. "The only difference is you still have this sweet innocence about you. She was a whore and drug addict but I still loved her all the same."

"What happened to her?"

"She died from a drug overdose."

"That's so sad."

"Life is sad that's why you have to embrace the moment," he said sprinkling my neck with kisses. Sway's touch instantly got me aroused. When his lips touched mine and then his tongue circulated inside my mouth, my pussy got wet and I wanted to step out of my panties and have him slide inside of me.

"Don't stop," I whispered as his tongue made its way to my hardened nipples. We were in a cabana at the W South Beach and right when I was ready to go all the way with Sway, Amir's face flashed in my mind. I opened my eyes and closed them back quickly trying to erase his image but it kept popping back up. "Wait!"

"What's wrong?"

"I'm a virgin. I'm not ready for this this to be my first time."

"Are you really about to play the virgin card? I like you. You don't have to do that."

"I'm not," I said, pushing him away. "I'm not telling you I'm a virgin so you'll like me. I'm telling you because it's true. And this doesn't feel right."

"You're serious?"

"Yes, I'm serious! Why the hell would I lie to you about something like that?"

"Because that's what a lot of women do. Thinking I'll like them more if they can get me to fall for their bullshit which they hope will enable them to get more out of me."

"You must not know who my people are. My father is Supreme also known as Xavier Mills. The original hip hop superstar turned music mogul. I drive a Lamborghini that my grandfather bought me as a birthday present. When I get back home I'll be staying at my other dad's estate in New Jersey. Let's not get this twisted. I enjoy your company but I don't need anything from you but a good time."

"Interesting, so you're one of those rich girls. No wonder you haven't asked me to pay any bills or take you shopping. And I thought it was all part of your MO to impress me."

"I'm going back to my room."

"Why?"

"Because I'm not in the mood for your analytical bullshit."

"You're so feisty."

"And you're so..." I yawned.

"Are you calling me boring?"

"Not you but this conversation is."

"I really like you, Aaliyah."

"You told me that already."

"This is a different, stronger feeling; but nothing has changed. I still want you. Even rich girls want to be taken care of. That's how they stay rich."

"I'm not ready yet to be with you like that."

"There's no rush for us to have sex. When we make love I need you to want to give me your body. If I can't have it like that then I don't want it." I found myself going right back to Sway but this time I was initiating the kisses. Something about him turned me on so much and it went beyond his celebrity good looks. His deep dark eyes seduced you with only a slight glance.

"I do want you," I admitted between kisses.

"What I'm not going to do is let you tease me. When you're ready for this dick, you'll give it up to me without hesitation until then we'll wait." Now Sway was pushing me away and it only made me want him more. This was one ride I should've gotten off a long time ago but now it was too late, I was already addicted.

Amir

Pandemonium

When I saw my dad and Nico come out the police station, I got out my car so I could find out once and for all what happened. "What did you find out?" I wasted no time in asking when they reached me.

"It's much more complicated than we thought." My dad's gravely tone sent a chill up my spine.

"What does that mean?"

"I'll let Nico explain." As Nico began to tell me what he found out from the police officers, my legs buckled and I almost fell to the ground but my car held me up. I heard what he was saying but I didn't want to believe it. My mind drifted back to what happened earlier that day.

"I can't decide what I'm wearing tonight to Sway's party. But I know I have to look extra cute."

"Justina, it's a party not the Inaugural Ball."

"It's not just a party. He's having it at that brand

new hotel in the city."

"What is he getting some suite?"

"No it's in the ballroom. I'm sure the after party will be in his suite and Aaliyah will be there no doubt. I still can't believe she's dating him."

"What are you talking 'bout? Aaliyah isn't dating Sway. She just did that modeling campaign with him and that was a one time deal."

"She swore me to secrecy but you're my boyfriend so I know you won't say anything."

"Say what?"

"Aaliyah doesn't want anybody to know. Her and Sway are dating and they have been for the last month. They're keeping it on the super low. The other day when we were at Nico's he sent her like a shit load of beautiful flowers. She showed me the card and they were from him."

"Aaliyah knows what type of nigga Sway is, she would never take him seriously."

"Are you kidding me! Sway Stone is rich, famous and hot looking why wouldn't she take him seriously. What girl in her right mind would turn him down!"

"Why do you always act like a fuckin' groupie when it comes to him!"

"Maybe because I'm a fan of his."

"Whatever, Justina. You go have fun at that little party you're dying to attend."

"You're not coming with me?"

"Nope."

"Why not?"

"Because I don't give a fuck about a Sway Stone

party. Go have a good time. I'll be here when you get back."

"Amir, you have to go."

"Why?"

"Because I'm not going to have anybody to talk to if you're not there."

"Aaliyah will be there."

"Yeah, all up under Sway."

"I'm sure Nichelle and Courtney will be there too."

"It's not the same. Amir, pleeeeeeease come with me. You're my boyfriend, you're supposed to be with me at things like this."

"Fine," I said reluctantly.

"Thank you, baby." Justina wrapped her arms around me and gave me a kiss. I kissed her back but my mind wasn't in it. I was too busy pondering what she said about Aaliyah and Sway. It fucked me up how my insides felt like they were about to explode knowing what was going on between them. I was wishing Lorenzo had killed him a long time ago but I had to get my emotions in check because I didn't want Justina to know that my feelings towards Aaliyah ran much deeper than just a friendship.

"No problem."

"So I'll get dressed and meet you back over here around seven."

"I have to go somewhere with my dad so I may not make it back here by then. Wait...here, take my key and let yourself in."

"You sure?"

"Definitely, it'll be nice coming home and have my

woman waiting for me."

"I like the sound of that." Justina whispered softly as if my bedroom was full of people and she wanted to make sure nobody heard her. "We still have a little bit of time before your dad gets home. We should take advantage of it." Before I could object Justina's Tunic dress was on the floor. She was standing in front of me in her bra and panties. "What are you waiting for?" Justina held out her hand and I reached out to take it.

"Nothing." I sat down on the edge of my bed and Justina stood between my legs. My hands caressed Justina's petite body and she leaned down to kiss me. Our tongues found each other but I was just going through the motions. Justina kissed my neck and took off my t-shirt before working her way down to my jeans. "Damn," I moaned out when I felt Justina's wet lips wrapped around my dick and her jaws and tongue worked its magic. Before I was about to bust in her mouth I laid her down on the bed."

"Amir, I love you." The look in her eyes showed that the words from her lips were true.

As I entered her flashes of Aaliyah's face took the place of Justina so I simply closed my eyes after saying, "I love you too."

When I got out the shower I glanced at the clock to see how much time I had before my dad was supposed to come back home. After we made love, Justina didn't want to leave. She stayed wrapped in my arms and

I didn't think it would be right for me to tell her to go until finally I didn't have a choice. Now I was rushing to get dressed because I planned to be ready when my dad got here. This was an important day for me. When I turned eighteen my dad promised he would begin showing me the ins and outs of his business as long as I promised to still go to college and get my degree. He said if I had a street degree and college degree I would be unstoppable. Today he was attending one of his monthly meetings and he was bringing me along. I had no idea what the meeting consisted of but it was important so I would be there.

After I got dressed I was headed towards the kitchen to get a bite to eat before we left but to my surprise my dad was already home. I could hear him talking loudly, and I figured he didn't know that I was home. I decided to keep it that way because I wanted to hear what was going on that had him so upset.

"You need to wait! How many times do I need to say that so you can understand!"

"Fuck that! That nigga is gon' die tonight. My people got everything set up. It's a go!"

"Lorenzo, we got too much other shit going on right now for you to move forward on killing that man."

"I can handle it and it will be handled because Sway Stone is dying tonight."

"You murder a high profile person like that it will bring too much heat. And we don't need that right now. We have to take care of these other snakes before you finish this out."

"Did you wait when you got retribution for the

people responsible for killing your wife?"

"Lorenzo, I understand where you're coming from and I have no problem with you handling things with Sway. Hell, I set your girl Courtney up with my sister so she could have a legitimate direct connect to Sway that you needed. Courtney has confirmed the suspicions you had about Sway and his involvement in Dior's death."

"Then what's the problem?"

"It's not the right time. Patience is not the enemy. Again, all I'm asking is that you wait until we get this one situation under control. Can you do that for me? Holding off for a couple weeks ain't gon' change shit. That nigga Sway will still be easy to find."

"I guess I can wait. Alexus and Lala have already been taken care of so I can be a little more patient when it comes to Sway. Especially since knowing he's six feet under will bring me the greatest gratification."

"You've made a wise decision. I know it's easy to get caught up in your emotions when it comes to loved ones but business always has to come first."

"You're right. We gotta sweep this other shit under the rug. Hopefully we'll make some headway at the meeting today."

"That's my hope. Speaking of the meeting, we need to get going. Let me call Amir and find out when he'll be home because I would hate to leave him. He's been asking to come with me today for the last couple of weeks."

For a quick second I couldn't decide if I should go to the front door and pretend I was just getting home, or go back to my bedroom so I made a hasty decision.

Knock...knock...knock

"Hey dad," I said pushing open the already half cracked door.

"Amir, I was just about to call you. When did you get home?"

"I've been home. After I took a shower I fell asleep. I just woke up. I figured I missed you, so I'm glad you didn't leave without me."

"You know I'm a man of my word. I told you, you can come. The only way it wouldn't happen is if you changed your mind."

"Nah, I wouldn't miss this for nothing. How can I miss going to a meeting with my dad and Lorenzo."

"Don't forget Nico. He'll also be joining us."

"Rolling with the three of you, I should learn a lot today."

"No doubt. You know your dad was reluctant about bringing you in but I believe you'll prove to him that he made the right decision."

"I will. This is something I want to be a part of."

"But remember, son, you have to hit those books. No school no being a part of the organization."

"I understand and I'm more than willing to do both."

"Good, now let's go because Nico's waiting downstairs."

When we got downstairs there were three black bullet proof SUV's waiting. Ever since I could remember, whenever he attended the once-a-month meeting, he would pull out these trucks and bring extra security. He said it was strictly a precaution because the meeting was attended by a group of high ranking drug kingpins from the east and west coast and although highly unlikely you could never be too careful. We all rode in the last SUV that Dice was driving. I felt like such a real man being in this circle. I even dressed the part. I would always see my dad, Nico and now Lorenzo who had been in the fold recently fitted in custom suits, designer ties and limited edition shoes so I made sure I represented as well. My YSL suite with a champagne tee had me looking important but not overdone.

During the drive everyone was pretty quiet. There was some small talk but my dad, Nico and Lorenzo were all either on their phones, texting or looking over paperwork. I was too anxious to do any of that plus my mind was also on Aaliyah and wondering what she was doing. I was tempted to send her a text but didn't want to get caught up in going back and forth texting her when making a positive impression at the meeting should be the only thing on the agenda. Also, I could relax my mind knowing that Sway Stone would be a dead man soon so the relationship didn't have a chance of surviving. As that thought entered my mind, I couldn't believe I was wishing death on another human being. I looked over at my father who was deep into his own world and I thought to myself that I could very well be a murderer just like him. Maybe I was more cut out for this business than either one of us knew.

After watching my father for a bit I turned my attention to Lorenzo who was texting nonstop. I immediately wondered if he was communicating with Precious.

I hadn't stopped shaking my head since finding out they were having a full fledge affair. The pain in Aaliyah's eyes when she found out still fucked with me. She knew shit was shaky with her parents but that just made the knife cut deeper in an already open wound. But I had to give her props for not blowing up and telling Supreme or Nico. Talk about a war breaking out. But like all secrets I knew eventually the shit would come out. I only hoped that Nico would be able to keep his cool and not want to kill Lorenzo, especially since they now did business together. Even though that relationship ended a long time ago, everybody knew that Nico was still in love with Precious and he tolerated her marriage to Supreme but accepting her being with Lorenzo that would cause more drama than any of us was ready for.

"We're here," I heard my dad say, snapping me out of visualizing Nico and Lorenzo going at it over Aaliyah's mom. When I glanced out the window we were parked in front of a nondescript brick building. The only reason anybody would know something serious was going down was because there were a dozen or so men dressed in security uniforms surrounding the spot.

"Is all this security really necessary," I commented to my dad before getting out the SUV. I found it amusing that each of them had on an NYPD baseball cap when they were doing security for criminals.

"Son, you're about to step into a room that's has over a billion dollars in it."

"Huh?"

"Combined, that's what we're worth. So yes all this security is justifiable." What my dad said fucked my head up. I knew I would be surrounded by official players in the game but the information he just dropped on me went beyond my expectations.

Upon entering the building everybody was searched and all cell phones were confiscated. Since the rules were implemented to protect them all nobody felt disrespected going through the security measures that seemed more appropriate for the airport. When we finally made it inside what appeared to be a poor man's establishment from the outside, it told a different story once you entered. The entrance had marble floors that made a direct path to a colossal board room. The majority of the chairs were already filled up and to my disbelief 'the board', as my dad called it was made up like the rainbow culture, from Black, White, Italian, Hispanic, Jamaican, Haitian and even an Asian man.

There were two waitresses walking around the table taking drink and or food order from the men. My dad had told me there was a chef on hand to cook whatever if anybody wanted to eat. My dad also told me that he never ate or drank anything at the meetings so I knew that meant I was supposed to follow his lead. Once we sat down we waited for a couple of other people to come in and take their seats and the meeting began with my father speaking.

"Good afternoon, gentleman."

"Good afternoon," they all said in unison. "Before we begin the meeting today, I wanted to introduce you to my son Amir." My dad motioned for me to stand up and I did speaking to everybody. "From here on out he will be attending our monthly meetings as he is now part of my organization. Does anybody have a problem with that?" Nobody objected and I figured my dad only asked the question as a form of respect not because he believed anyone would oppose.

"Welcome," a white man sitting across from me said, and one by one the others gave me the same single word greeting. Once I sat back down my father continued.

"Everybody here today is extremely busy so let's get right to it. The first order of business is deciding who will take over the Queens territory now that Miguel is deceased.

"Has his family got back with you about what they want to do?" The heavy set Hispanic man who was sitting on the far right questioned.

"Yes, his family doesn't want to continue on in the business. They are basically looking for a buyout. They want to be well compensated as we're all aware it's a very profitable territory."

"I want it," the Asian man said casually lifting up his index finger.

"I want it too," the white man that was first to welcome me, let it be known.

"It should be mine," the heavy set Hispanic man bellowed out and just like that bickering began. And here I thought only women did that but these men who all seemed so calm and reserved started going at it. I now understood why they were frisked at the door because this room was about money and if anybody got in their way of making it, it quickly turned ugly.

"Gentleman, calm down," my dad said quietly but

they continued on, yelling at each other and arguing why they deserved it more than the next person. "Calm it down!" My dad yelled out when the men still hadn't regained their composure. After my dad got their attention they all began squirming in their seats trying to contain their anger. "I understand that most of you would like to take over Miguel's territory but it isn't possible. Like we do with everything else we'll handle it professionally. Each one of you that would like to make an offer on the territory, explain why you feel it will be in all of our benefit to allow you to take it over. Once you've done so then we'll vote. Whatever the final result is, everybody will respect it and abide by it, agreed."

"Agreed," they all echoed.

I sat back and listened to six out of the fifteen men on the board tell why it would be the best decision for everyone involved to allow them to have the territory. Although it was obvious each man was aggravated with the other they all managed to keep their poise. Watching how they conducted their meeting let me know that any of these men could run a Fortune 500 company with their eyes closed. They were negotiating and pleading their cases better than top attorneys in multi-million dollar firms. I was learning more observing them than I would ever learn in a top university with the best professors. This shit right here was intoxicating.

"Thank you gentleman, unless anybody has any further questions it's time to vote." The men all nodded their head in agreement and then some high tech miniature screen popped up from the table that allowed everyone to place their private vote. I was looking forward to knowing who nailed it and when the results popped up on the main flat screen above the fireplace, I smiled seeing Nico had won.

"Bloodfire! Mi always inna crosses when it comes to voting in these meetings," the Jamaican man blurted out. Everybody ignored his comment as if they were used to him lashing out every time he loss, which I figured from what he said, often.

"Joder!" The Hispanic belted out and pounded his fist on the mahogany table.

"Relax, Jose. You can't always win. I lost this one too. What Nico said made more sense for the overall operation. As a matter of fact your argument was basically pointless," the white man said without hesitation.

"Que te jodan! Me cago en la madre que te pario." The white man gave Jose a blank stare because clearly he didn't understand a word he said which was a good thing. I took Spanish in school and not only did he say fuck you, he also said he would shit on the mother that gave birth to him. Those were fighting words for most of the people I knew.

"If you have something to say, Jose, I would appreciate it if you used English. That is the language we all comprehend in here."

Jose glared at the white man and spit, "Hijo de puta," and folded his arms.

"This issue took much longer than expected so unless anybody has any pertinent business issues that can't wait to be addressed at next month's meeting then we'll bring this to a close." With the way tempers were flaring that was a wise move on my dad's behalf to end this shit now and everybody else seemed to agree the way they were hauling ass to get out of there. A couple of men stopped and congratulated Nico on his win but most left with aggravation etched on their face.

"That worked out well," my dad commented as we were walking out. With all three of them being in business together, with Nico winning it benefited them just as much. I had a feeling they already strategized what they planned on doing a while ago. So it made sense that neither my dad nor Lorenzo jumped in on the bidding. They out slicked the slickers. The three of them were in deep conversation as we walked out the building. From the entry I saw all the board members waiting out front for their cars to pull up. I then noticed Dice getting out the SUV opening the door for us and the other two SUVs with the additional armed bodyguards behind him. As we were retrieving our cell phones from one of the security officers, I did a double take. At first I thought I was mistaken but when I looked back again I realized that I wasn't. He had on a black cap but it didn't have the NYPD on it and he was also wearing black gloves and black shades. I prided myself on having an excellent memory and none of the men I saw had those three things on when we first arrived. I was praying that I was wrong but I decided to follow my gut.

"Dad," I yelled out in a not so loud tone not wanting to bring any additional attention on us.

"What is it, Amir?" he slightly turned around and asked.

"I don't want to see the shining stars." My dad's

eyes widened as he swiftly did an assessment of the surrounding area. That was our secret code phrase and we only used it when we believed our life was in jeopardy. When I was little I would always say that I don't want to see the shining stars because that meant it was dark and I couldn't stay outside and play any longer because it was time to get ready for bed. When I got older my dad made it our secret code because nobody would ever know to say that but us.

"Code silver," he screamed out repeatedly and I watched Dice say it through his earpiece. Right when Dice, and the armed guards stepped out with weapons aimed we heard the sound of gunshots spraying the afternoon air. My dad ran towards me grabbing my arm to make sure we both made it to the bullet proof truck. We all practically dived inside the open door for cover. Once inside I looked out the window and saw body after body dropping to the ground. It was about a dozen of the bootleg security men saturating bodies with bullets and none of them had on the NYPD hats. I realized they must've taken them all out while we were inside having our meeting. They were definitely top notch hired goons because it seemed their shots never missed the intended mark. All I could do was thank God my dad made sure we came in bullet proof SUVs and I knew the rest of the board members wished they had done the same.

"Dice, come on! We need to get the fuck outta here," Nico barked. Saying what the rest of us were thinking. Between the time Dice was reloading his weapon and making his way to the driver's side, I witnessed his brain splatter against the window. It literally happened that fast. I didn't even have time to dwell on it because with Dice down I knew somebody had to drive so I stepped up and did it myself.

"Amir!" My dad screamed but I ignored him. I was close to the front driver's seat so I did what I had to do. Luckily Dice had left the engine running so all I had to do was press down on the gas and be out. I wasn't stopping for nothing and anybody in my way was getting ran the fuck over.

"Yo, who the fuck set this shit up! It's a fuckin' bloodbath out there. I couldn't even tell if anybody survived," Nico said in disbeif.

"Yeah, it's bad, and Dice, he was a good man."

"Genesis, who do you think could've put a green light on this."

"I have no fuckin' idea. But I will find out. Amir, first drive through the car wash and then head to the apartment."

"Are you sure? I mean about the part of us going back to the apartment."

"I'm positive. I wouldn't tell you to if I wasn't. Lorenzo, hand me that cell phone under the seat." From the mirror I could see Lorenzo toss my dad the phone and he immediately made a call. "Meet me at my apartment. Have someone do a thorough walk through and leave three men posted downstairs to monitor any suspicious activity. Also, I need two fully loaded cars waiting for my arrival which will be within the hour."

"Genesis, do you think this has anything to do with the man Tony had been dealing with, Dale? If that's even his name."

"I don't know what to think right now. But I'm going to make moves like our operation is under attack. Amir, if everything is clear then I'm going to drop you off at the apartment while we find out who had the fuckin' balls to give clearance to this bullshit."

"Dad, I want to come with you."

"I know. If I had any doubts about your capabilities and whether you had the heart to be a member of this organization you've squashed them. You will be a great asset but as your leader when I give a command, don't question it just follow it."

"Yes Sir." I remained silent for the duration of the drive and simply listened. Often you could learn a lot more that way.

When I turned on Lexington Avenue and pulled up in front of our apartment building I noticed the security team. They were discreetly dressed in street clothes so they wouldn't stand out but we knew exactly who they were. "I'll be right back," my dad said getting out the car.

When I turned to look for my keys in the front passenger seat I noticed Aaliyah going inside of my building. She came from the opposite direction so she couldn't have noticed us. Plus the tint on this truck was so dark she wouldn't have been able to see who was inside anyway. As I was debating if I should call her and tell her it wasn't a good time to come see me my dad came back to the car.

"Everything is clear. So, Amir, you go upstairs. I'm sure you already know this but don't discuss what happened today with anybody. I'll speak with you later on."

"Ok, but dad, can I have the key to the apartment? I don't have mine on me."

"Sure, here you go." After my dad handed me his key I got out and watched as he, Nico and Lorenzo got into one of the other vehicles. A member of the security team got behind the wheel of the truck I was driving and drove off. It was burning me up that I wasn't continuing on with my dad and them. I wanted to be right there in the mix but like he told me, part of being a member of the operation is following commands, so I would prove to him I could do just that. I knew if I did, my time would come.

I hurried to get upstairs to meet Aaliyah. Even with the chaos that went on today I was looking forward to seeing her. When the elevator doors opened there she was and when I saw her face, I instantly thought about what was going on with her and Sway so I became irritated. "Amir, I was just about to leave."

"Glad I caught you."

"Where are you coming from?"

"I made a run with my dad."

"Oh, is he on his way up?"

"No, he dropped me off. He has some business to handle," I explained opening the door to the penthouse. "I'm surprised to see you here. I thought you would be with Sway."

"Sway, why would you think that? That's a stupid question. I guess pillow talk got the best of Justina."

"So why didn't you tell me?" By the time we reached my bedroom Aaliyah still hadn't answered me.

"Why didn't you tell me, Aaliyah," I persisted wanting her to give me an answer.

"I don't know. Maybe because I knew you wouldn't approve."

"Are you sleeping with him?"

"That's a bold question."

"Answer it."

"Why do you care?"

"Because I want to know. I hope you weren't dumb enough to lose your virginity to him like you planned on doing with D'Mario."

"Wow, that was a low blow, even for you, Amir."

"What's low is that you're even dating that loser. So have you fucked him or not?"

"No! Not that it's any of your fuckin' business. But so you know, I will be fuckin' him tonight after his party."

"I'm not surprised you're willing to whore yourself out to Sway Stone. Two narcissists like you belong together."

"I can't believe how cruel you're being to me. And to think I came over here to tell you I need one more chance."

"One more chance to what, try and fuck up my life. In one breath you're telling me you're planning on fuckin' another nigga tonight and then next you're asking me for another chance...classic Aaliyah behavior. You're so fuckin' self-absorbed it's nauseating."

"You're not holding back any punches today, that's for sure." I could see Aaliyah fighting to not let her tears escape but I couldn't stop myself from beating up on her with my words. My dad was right, I was so in love with her but I refused to let myself give into my feelings even if I had to tear her down to do so.

"All I'm doing is telling the truth. The best thing I ever did was make sure things never went further than a kiss between us."

"You win. If it was your goal to make me feel like the lowest piece of shit, you've accomplished it."

"You should!" Aaliyah and I both turned our head and saw Justina standing in the doorway.

"Fuck," I said under my breath, remembering that Justina had told me she was coming over so we could go to Sway's party together.

"I come over early to wait for my boyfriend and I find out him and my so called best friend shared a kiss."

"Justina, it's not what you think."

"Shut up, Aaliyah! I heard everything! And you are a narcissist and self-absorbed. I couldn't have picked better words to describe you. You've been throwing yourself at Amir all this time."

"Justina, despite what you heard that's not true."

"Are you really standing there about to defend her, Amir? You said it yourself, she's a whore."

"That's not what I said."

"I get it. You're the only one that can talk shit to Aaliyah but she's off limits to everybody else."

"You have every right to be upset. And I'm sorry. Amir is your boyfriend which makes him off limits. But you have to understand, I've been in love with him for just as long as you have."

"You don't love anybody but yourself, Aaliyah. You've always been that way since I can remember. All the attention has to be on you. Getting all that love and attention from two dads and a grandfather isn't enough for you. Dating fuckin' Sway Stone isn't even enough for you. You have to have Amir too. Is that who you've been saving your virginity for, my boyfriend? How can a non dick getting virgin be the worse type of whore I know?"

"That's enough, Justina."

"It's okay."

"Oh please, Aaliyah, don't start trying to play the victim now."

"I'm not. I just have no interest in continuing to stand here and listen to you and Amir basically paint me as the worse human being ever. I apologize, Justina, I crossed the line and it'll never happen again. I'm going to the party tonight with Sway and hopefully I'll see the two of you there and we can forget what just happened. The three of us have been best friends for as long as I can remember and I don't want that to change."

"I don't think you're the worse person ever, Aaliyah. I shouldn't have said those things to you, it was wrong."

"Thank you, Amir."

"What the hell is wrong with you? Are you in love with her too, Amir?"

"I'ma leave the two of you alone. Justina, I hope you can forgive me." There was complete silence in my bedroom until we heard the door shut when Aaliyah left.

"Amir, are you in love with, Aaliyah?" Justina asked again not letting it go.

"Of course I love her. I've known her all my life."

"You know that's not what I asked you."

"Yes, I'm in love with Aaliyah. But I do love you too, Justina."

"Yeah, you love me but you're in love with Aaliyah."

"I am." There was no sense in denying my feelings but I was expressing them to the wrong person.

"So what about us, Amir?"

"I'm trying to figure it all out. I need some time to do that."

"Fine, take all the time you need. But while you're doing that, remember all the reasons you chose not to be with Aaliyah in the first place."

When Justina left I sat down on my bed and did just that. I kept battling myself on whether I should or shouldn't pursue a relationship with Aaliyah. Yeah, I was in love with her but was it enough to make it work? That was what I needed to decide.

Aaliyah

The Show, The After-Party, The Hotel

"Aaliyah, I need you to tell me exactly what happened last night," the attorney my dad had hired asked me. I had been begging for some type of representation all night but now that I had it this fear was suffocating me. A fear of exposing all that happened and it wasn't pretty.

"Are you going to be able to get me out on bail?"

"You're charged with first degree murder so it will be difficult but at the arraignment I'll argue the state doesn't have sufficient evidence for that charge and we'll go from there."

"That doesn't sound promising."

"Aaliyah, I'm the best. That's why your father hired me and your mother is in agreement that I represent you. I need you to trust me."

"So what do I need to do?"

"Tell me what happened and don't leave anything out. I don't care how insignificant you think it might be. Whatever you reveal is protected under client/attorney privilege." I sat back in my chair and began to tell my story, the truth, and the whole truth so help me God.

"Aaliyah, what time will you be home tonight?"

"I don't know."

"You don't know."

"That's what I said."

"Where are you going, smart ass."

"A party."

"Can you quit with these two and three word answers."

"I'm going to Sway's party. First he's doing an intimate show, then an after-party at a hotel ballroom in the city."

"Who are you going with?"

"The usual suspects."

"You mean Justina and Amir."

"That's them," I lied. I was hoping they would both come but after our blowout I seriously doubted it.

"After the party I want you to come home."

"Why? I might decide to spend the night in the city. The party isn't going to be over until late."

"You've been on the road traveling for the last few weeks."

"I was working."

"I know and now the modeling gig is up. You'll be starting college soon and it's time for you to start focusing on that."

"Ok, but I don't need to come home after the party to do that."

"I'm not trying to give you a hard time. I would prefer if you came home after the party."

"I tell you what. I promise I will try to leave the party early enough that I can make it home. Does that work?"

"I know you're eighteen and you feel like you're grown. I remember being that age I met Supreme around the same time. He was this huge star just like Sway is. But your father was always grounded, much more so than me."

"Can you get to the point?"

"Sway may have your father's fame but he doesn't have his character."

"What are you talking about?"

"I had him checked out and he's trouble, Aaliyah."

"I'm going to his party. We're not walking down the aisle."

"I just don't want you to make the same bad choices you made with D'Mario, you remember what happened with that."

"How can I forget! You constantly remind me of it every chance you get. Since we're playing the reminder game, have you worked out that little situation you have going on with Lorenzo yet?"

"Aaliyah, this isn't about Lorenzo."

"But now I'm completely curious. Normally you never like to spend the entire summer in New Jersey and New York but for some reason things has changed this year. Is it because Lorenzo is here and you want to be closer? You have it all figured out, mother. Daddy, right here in the house, Lorenzo across the river, must be nice. I want to be just like you when I grow up."

"I told you before that I wasn't discussing my relationship with Lorenzo with you anymore and I'm asking you again to respect that."

"I will but can you do the same and respect my relationship with Sway and not ask me about it? I think you're playing with fire by seeing Lorenzo. Not only are you married but he's a criminal. Since you like checking people out I'm sure you did research on your own man."

"You keep making this about me when it's really about you. You're young with your whole life ahead of you. A few bad decisions are all it takes to ruin everything."

"They're my bad decisions to make. You made mistakes and you survived them and I will too. If you keep trying to hinder me from living my life and learning from the errors I make you're going to alienate me."

"Fine, Aaliyah. I'll give you your space. But I'm not going to stop being your mother. And that means if I feel you're going down the wrong path I'm going to tell you. Whether you decide to take my advice is up to you."

"That's fair."

"Enjoy the party tonight but if you need me I'm only a phone call away."

"Thank you." I closed my bedroom door after my mother said her piece. I knew she meant well but I didn't want to hear it. I wanted to do what I wanted to do if only for tonight and I would.

Sway was still blowing up my phone as I arrived at the hotel on Columbus Circle. I missed his show and was late for his party. The conversation with my mother left me in a funk so instead of rushing to get ready I took my time and then some more time before I knew it was a couple hours later. When I entered the hotel lobby Sway called me again but this time I answered.

"Hello."

"Where are you?"

"I just walked in the hotel."

"Come upstairs. I left a room key at the front desk in your name."

"Ok, I'm on my way up." I stopped by the front desk and like Sway said they had a room key for me. I took the elevator and got off on the 53rd floor for the Presidential Suite. I had been in so many different hotels these last few weeks that they all were starting to look the same to me. When I got to the room at first I knocked but then I remembered I had the key and opened the door. I could hear the television but I didn't see Sway. I walked in the dining and living room area and there he was standing in front of the window, looking out at the panoramic view of Central Park and The City.

"I'm glad you were finally able to make it," Sway stated without diverting from the view.

"I apologize for missing your show. I got caught up at home."

"I understand." He finally turned around as he spoke to me. "You look beautiful. The color of the dress compliments your skin tone." I knew he was telling the truth because the main reason I picked out the metallic one-shoulder mini dress was because the way it made my caramel color pop.

"Thank you. Too bad I was late for the show and party because nobody gets to see it but you."

"Aren't I the only one that matters?"

"It was a joke, Sway. So are we staying in for the rest of the night?" Before he responded I heard the bathroom door open. "What the hell are you doing here?"

"Sway invited me up."

"Oh really," I spit eyeing Sway.

"You were taking so long he needed someone to keep him company."

"Justina, this is pathetic. What, you're going to throw some pussy at Sway to get back at me and Amir."

"I'm not throwing anything anywhere. Sway invited me up to his room."

"Yeah, I'm sure after you gave him an earful. But fine, if you want to fuck Sway, be my guest. I'm not entertaining this bullshit." I left the key on the table and turned around to leave.

"Aaliyah, wait. I have no intention of fucking Justina."

"Then what is she doing here?"

"She came to the party alone. You weren't there and we started to talk."

"Well, I'm here now so she can go."

"You think you run everything, Aaliyah, but you don't. Did you tell Sway how you threw yourself at my boyfriend earlier today."

"I didn't throw myself at Amir. We had a conversation that you caught a part of. I told you I was sorry."

"You think because you say sorry it makes all the damage you've done disappear but it doesn't. It's time that you're held accountable for the bitch that you are."

"And you're the person that's going to hold me accountable? You're so ungrateful. I regret that I ever gave you that makeover. That's when you turned into this I'm the shit you can't tell me anything Justina. But with all the makeup and new clothes you're still that mousey French braid wearing girl living through me. Get over yourself. I never claimed to be perfect. I made a mistake but you trying to fuck Sway isn't going to change that. Now please get your shit and get out of here!"

"Sway doesn't want me to leave." Justina said, staggering to the table pouring a glass of champagne.

"Is that true, Sway?"

"Of course it's true. What you think a man like Sway wouldn't want me?"

"Are you drunk, Justina?"

"I'm fine! You're the one who's uptight. Maybe this will relax you." Before I could blink, Justina had picked up the bottle of champagne and poured it in my face, hair and dress. My natural reflex kicked in and I yanked Justina up by her neck. As she yanked her head to get out of my grasp my nails scraped across her neck drawing blood.

"Aaliyah, calm down." Sway came over and held me back as I was about to start swinging on Justina. "Go in the bathroom and clean yourself up. You can take off your dress and put this on," he said handing me one of his shirts. "I'll get some ice for Justina's neck." It took me a moment to move but I finally took Sway's advice and went to clean up.

When I entered the bathroom the outfitted honey onyx walls seemed to calm my nerves, which Justina had totally worked over. I slipped off my champagne drenched dress and then stared at myself in the mirror. My hair was soaked in champagne and the only way to get rid of the smell was to wash it. I stepped in the glass enclosed steam shower and turned on the hot water. As I washed the smell off me I kept thinking about how reckless Justina's behavior was. I wanted to stay in the shower for as long as possible hoping by the time I got out Sway would've gotten rid of her.

The longer I stayed in the shower the more I thought about Justina. I understood she was angry about Amir but she had taken things way too far. But she was still like a sister to me so I decided when I got out the shower I would call Amir and tell him to come pick her up. She was tipsy and as pissed as I was with her I wanted her to get home safely. I got out the shower, dried myself off and put on the shirt Sway gave me. I was dreading having to see Justina after what she did but at least now I felt clean. When I opened the bathroom door it was pitch black. I couldn't see anything.

"Sway, turn on the light." But I got no response so I went back in the bathroom to turn the light on and that's when I felt a hard bump on my head and fell out.

I shook my head as I tried regaining my focus. I didn't know how long I had been out of it but my head was hurting. When I rubbed it I realized I had gloves on and I was holding something. I still couldn't regain my center.

It took me what felt like ten or fifteen minutes to fully regain consciousness. As soon as I did I saw that what I had in my hand was a gun. Then I got scared because I assumed if I was holding a gun somebody must've tried to hurt me.

The lights were all still off so I felt my way around and in the process I tripped over something but got right back up. When I reached the light switch I turned it on, and that's when the nightmare began. Sway was sprawled out across the bed with a bullet in his head and Justina was on the floor with a bullet in her chest. I panicked. I had these gloves on, I was holding a gun and the only person I could think to call was Amir. I looked for my purse so I could get my cell phone. I called him and at first he didn't answer so I called again. But right when he answered the police were coming into the hotel room with guns aimed at me saying I was under arrest.

"Hello."

"Amir, it's me! I'm about to get arrested for murder!" That's all I could get out before the police took my cell phone and handcuffed me as they read me my rights.

"So that's all you remember?" my attorney asked after I finished telling him what happened that fatal night.

"Yes."

"You're not leaving out anything?"

"No. I'm telling you that's what happened.

Somebody set me up for those murders."

"It's only one murder so far. Justina is in critical condition."

"Do you think she'll pull through? She's my only hope."

"I don't know. But she's not your only hope. If Justina wakes up and can identify the shooter as not being you, then she's your quickest hope but not your only."

"Does the fact that I have this bump on my head help?"

"The prosecutor will argue that you got it while fighting with Justina. You admit to scratching her and having an altercation so that won't help but trust me there is always evidence that will work in your favor. And that's what I'm paid to do, find it."

"So when will I get out?"

"That's the next thing I'll be working on but I wanted to speak to you first to prepare."

"What am I supposed to do until you find out if a bail will be set?"

"Stay calm and quiet. Don't talk to anybody about your case. I will be able to get you a visit with your parents, which will hopefully make you feel better."

"What about my grandfather. Can I see him? He always makes me feel better."

"Quentin is on a flight as we speak. But when he gets here you will be able to see him. Maybe by that time you might be out on bail."

"Mr. Anderson, is that a real possibility?"

"Call me Pete, and yes, with me as your attorney, anything is possible."

With Pete Anderson as my attorney anything is possible, I kept repeating to myself as I was taken back to my jail cell. It was all I had right now and that Justina had survived. But I couldn't wrap my mind around the fact that Sway Stone was dead and the world would believe I was his killer. Maybe for now it was better I stayed locked up in jail I thought shaking my head.

Amir

Set Fire to The Rain

I sat in Justina's hospital room praying she would wake up. I held her hand and it seemed there was no life left in it. But I had to believe she would pull through and get better, she had to. She had to let the detectives know that Aaliyah wasn't responsible for her lying in a coma or for Sway Stone's murder. It wasn't any way possible she was capable of murdering her best friend no matter what went down between them. I couldn't help but feel guilty about both of their predicaments. As I thought back to what happened the day of Sway's party a huge burden fell on me. It was because of me they argued and I prayed Aaliyah and Justina would get through this. But I knew whatever the outcome things would never be the same between the three of us again.

"How is she?" my dad asked when he came in Justina's room.

"No change."

"This is unfortunate. Justina's in a coma and Aaliyah is in jail. How does something like this happen?

I don't understand."

"Dad, can we talk out in the hallway for a minute?"

"Sure."

"I need to ask you a question," I told my dad when we found a private area in the hospital.

"What is it?"

"The day of Sway's party I heard a conversation between you and Lorenzo." I kept my voice low not wanting anybody to hear what my dad and I were discussing.

"Okay." That's all my dad said not giving up nothing until he knew where I was going with my dialogue.

"Lorenzo said he planned on moving forward with killing Sway that night and you pleaded with him not to."

"Where are you going with this, Amir?"

"Is it possible that Lorenzo didn't do what you asked and went ahead and let his people move forward with the hit?"

"Are you insinuating that Lorenzo is responsible for Justina being in that coma?"

"All I'm saying is that he was adamant that Sway's death happen that night. Is it possible he made sure it did?"

"It's possible that I could've killed Sway and shot Justina but I didn't. Possibilities are endless, Amir, that's what makes life so powerful. But one thing I know about Lorenzo is if he tells me he'll wait then that's what he'll do."

"Can you at least ask him and see what he says? Aaliyah is locked up because of this."

"Amir, I love Aaliyah too. Do you think I would

allow Nico's daughter who is family to me, stay locked up in jail if there was something I could do about it."

"There is something you can do."

"Amir, I know how you feel about Aaliyah. I've always known but you can't alienate vital people in my operation because you want to hurry up and get her out. Nico has the best attorney money can buy on her case. Quentin's influence reaches long and wide. But I've told you before and I'll tell you again, you have to keep your emotions in check. Do you understand?"

"Yes."

"Good. Now I will talk to Lorenzo and I'll let you know what I find out. But I do have some information on that hit. There's a war going on over the Bronx operation, based along a 30-block corridor of White Plains Road and a Far Rockaway street gang is heavily involved. They may be responsible for what happened as a way to get rid of all the competition and at the same time place all the blame on their rival so everybody will go after them. That way they end up with the Bronx spot plus snatch up everything else."

"So what are we going to do?"

"Wipe them out first and if need be take out both sides that way we leave nobody standing."

"When are you planning the attack?"

"We're going to lay low for a little while because of what happened everybody is on the defense. Let them ease up until they think the dogs have fallen back into a deep sleep then we make our move."

"Got it."

"I have to take care of some things, so I'll see you

later on at home."

"Ok."

I stopped by Justina's room again before heading out. It was getting late and I needed to go home and try to get some rest. I hadn't gotten any sleep since everything went down and at the rate things were going, I wouldn't be getting much anytime soon. I kissed Justina's forehead and prayed when I came back tomorrow she would be awake.

Ring...Ring...Ring

I was so exhausted I barely heard my cell ringing. "Hello," I groaned in the phone.

"Amir, it's me."

"Aaliyah!" Hearing her voice prompted me to wake right up.

"I just got out on bail."

"You did! Where are you?"

"On my way to my dad's house."

"I'm on the way." I jumped up and got in the shower. I was dying to see Aaliyah. My dad had told me that her family would get her out and I was relieved he was right. Now I just wanted her to know that I was in her corner. I couldn't get dressed quick enough. When I was done I grabbed my car keys and headed out.

"Where are you rushing out to?" I ran into my dad as he was coming out his office.

"Aaliyah called me. You were right. The attorney

Bitch

Nico hired got her out."

"I told you he would. So you're going to see her?"

"Yeah, she said she was on her to way to Nico's house."

"That's good. I also had an opportunity to speak with Lorenzo."

"What did he say?"

"He told his people to hold off on the Sway murder. They were nowhere near the hotel when Sway and Justina were shot."

"Thanks for asking him dad."

"No problem. But when you go see Aaliyah all you need to do is reassure her that everything will be okay and she has your support."

"That's what I plan on doing."

"Give Aaliyah my best."

"I will."

"Amir, come in," Nico opened the door and it was a mini family reunion. Quentin, Precious, Supreme and Xavier were all there. The only person missing was Aaliyah.

"Where's Aaliyah?"

"I know how much she wanted to see you but when she went upstairs to lie down for a little while she passed out. She probably didn't sleep at all when she was in jail."

"I'm sure you're right, Mrs. Mills. If she does wake up will you tell her to call me?"

207

"Of course. She's going to be so disappointed that she missed you."

"She needs to get her rest. I'll be back."

"How's Justina?"

"Still the same. But I'm on my way to the hospital so hopefully there's been a change but you know I'll keep you informed on the latest."

"Thank you. That means a lot to me, Amir."

"No problem." I gave Aaliyah's mom an encouraging smile because I could see how worried she was. "Bye everybody," I put my hand up and walked out the door.

I left the house with emptiness in my heart. I had wanted to hold Aaliyah, tell her that I love her but I would have to be patient. Soon I could speak from my heart and Aaliyah and I would get through this together.

Aaliyah

Rebirth

When I woke up, the first thing I did was get out of bed and opened the French doors that led to my balcony overlooking the pool and the flowing fountains. Ever since I was a little girl, I loved water. As I grew up it always seemed to soothe my mind and give me a sense of calmness, which I needed more than anything right now. I was finally out free on bail but I felt more like a prisoner now than when I was locked up.

Overnight I had become infamous for being the girl who murdered Superstar Sway Stone. Every newspaper had my face splashed across it and I continued to be the #1 trending topic on Twitter even ahead of Sway's actual death. I was the breaking news for every media outlet and it was all for a murder I did not commit, but no one seemed to believe me. Even worse was the attempted murder charge for Justina. She was like my sister and for what happened that night in Sway's suite to be betrayed as a lover's quarrel gone wrong was killing me softly.

Escaping to my dad's estate in New Jersey helped

some because being in New York was out the question. It gave the paparazzi and media too much easy access to me but many were willing to go through a tunnel or cross a bridge to stalk me. But my dad did have plenty of security guarding his home so it did give me a certain level of comfort. As I gazed out into the clear blue skies without a cloud in sight, I wondered how something so beautiful made me feel such misery. I then started to pretend that my current predicament wasn't real, that I was actually vacationing on a beachfront villa, sipping a pina colada. I was so caught up in my daydreaming it took me a minute to hear someone knocking on my bedroom door.

"Just a minute," I called out. "Hey," I said opening the door and seeing my dad standing there.

"Good morning, can I come in?"

"Of course."

"I was worried. I was knocking on your door for a few minutes."

"I apologize. I was outside on the balcony dreaming I was someplace else and didn't hear you."

"You don't want to stay here with me?"

"No, dad, that came out wrong. I meant someplace else like not wanting to stay locked up in my bedroom because I have this murder charge hanging over my head. I wish none of this was real."

"Me too, but it is. Your attorney wanted to come over this afternoon to further discuss the case. Are you up for it?"

"No but I don't have much of a choice. This is really happening to me," I said with my voice trembling.

I sat down on my bed shaking my head in disbelief. "Any news on Justina?"

"She's still in a coma."

"If only Justina would wake up. She would tell everybody that it wasn't me and this nightmare would end."

"But there is a chance she won't wake up so we have to prepare for that. That's why you have to meet with your attorney so he can begin the process of preparing your case. You need a defense."

"What do you mean? I have a defense...I didn't do it!"

"I know that's what you're saying, but..."

"What do you mean, that's what I'm saying!" I screamed cutting my dad off. "You don't believe me?"

"Aaliyah, I never said I didn't believe you."

"And you never said that you do. Out of everybody I just assumed you would be the one person that believed me."

"Of course I believe you," he said coming over and wrapping his arms around me.

"Get off of me," I screamed pushing him away. "You're like everybody else; you think I'm a murderer. I can even tell mom isn't sure if I did it or not."

"That is not true. Precious is on your side."

"Of course she's on my side. She doesn't want to see her only daughter locked away and spending the rest of her life in jail but that doesn't mean she thinks I'm innocent. But daddy, I swear to you, I didn't do this. You have to believe me," I cried out.

"My sweet baby girl, I do," my dad reassured me as

he held me tightly. My body was shaking uncontrollably as my reality set in. "We'll get through this as a family."

"I don't want to go back there. I don't won't to spend the rest of my life in jail."

"And you won't. I promise. I don't care what I have to do you will not spend the rest of your life in jail." My dad held me until I calmed down. His assertion was giving me strength. "I love you," he said, kissing my forehead. "We all love you and believe in your innocence."

"Thank you, daddy. I'm sorry for yelling at you earlier."

"Don't apologize. What you're going through is tough. But my blood and your mother's blood run through you, so you're a warrior. You'll not only get through this but you'll beat it and come out stronger than you've ever imagined."

"You're right."

"I know. Now relax your mind and get ready to meet with your attorney, okay."

"Okay, and daddy..."

"Yes," he stopped and turned around as he was walking out.

"I love you too." He smiled and for the first time since this nightmare begun I was filled with hope and not despair. A smiled even crept across my face and I was about to go take a shower, I heard my cell ringing. I looked at the screen and saw it was Amir.

"Hey. I'm sorry I missed you yesterday. But I was so tired. When I got home as soon as I hit the bed I fell asleep."

"Don't apologize. You've been through a lot. How

are you?"

"I'm feeling better. Just had a conversation with my dad and I'm a lot more optimistic."

"Glad to hear that. I have some news that should make you feel even more optimistic."

"What is it?" I didn't even try to conceal the excitement in my voice because I needed all the good news I could get.

"Justina's condition is improving."

"Is she out the coma?"

"When I came in this morning the doctor said she's been opening her eyes and trying to talk."

"This is just the sort of news I needed to hear!"

"Yeah, everybody including the doctor believes the worse is over."

"This is great! Did you ask her about what happened?"

"She wasn't awake that long. They really didn't have a chance to talk to her because soon after she fell asleep."

"When will she wake back up?"

"Aaliyah, I don't know. See that's why I really didn't want to tell you because I knew you would have all these questions that I don't know the answer to. But the important thing is Justina is out of her coma and soon she'll be able to clear your name."

"Thank you, Amir. At first I wasn't sure if you believed me but I can hear it in your voice that you do."

"I've always believed you. I know you're not capable of what they're charging you with. I'm going to stay here with Justina in case she wakes up again. But tomorrow morning before I head back to the hospital I'm going to come over and take you out for breakfast."

"I don't think I'm ready to go out yet."

"You need to leave the house."

"We'll see. I would love your company though. If I'm not up for going out we can have breakfast out by the pool."

"That works. I'll call you later if there are any updates with Justina but regardless I'll see you tomorrow morning."

"Looking forward to it. Bye." When I hung up with Amir I screamed out, "Yes!" In a short span of time, things were already turning around in my favor.

When I went in the bathroom and looked at myself in the mirror, I finally found life again. My sparkling green eyes that I inherited from my grandmother had seemed vacant once my pampered life was turned upside down. I wasn't sure if that vivacity would ever appear again but after my phone call with Amir, now I was positive it would.

After a long hot shower I went downstairs and was pleasantly surprised to see my mother downstairs in the living room talking with my dad. I had no idea she was coming back over so soon but I was happy because I could now share the good news with them at the same time. I stood back and watched them interact for a second. I had never paid attention to it before but I could see there was so much love between them. It didn't matter though because my mother was married to my dad and seemed to still be in love with Lorenzo.

"Aaliyah, why are you just standing there? Come give me a hug," my mother said when she noticed me.

"I didn't want to interrupt you and daddy."

"I missed you," my mother said giving me a hug. "I know I saw you yesterday but we didn't spend that much time together because you went right to sleep."

"Nico, told me your attorney is on his way over to discuss your case some more. But I was hoping when he's done you can come home with me for a few days. Instead of staying at the apartment in the city we can stay at the house in Saddle River."

"I can do that."

"Really!"

"Yes," I smiled.

"I'm so glad to hear you say that. I was telling Nico you were going to fight me on it. It's a relief that you're not."

"But can it be tomorrow instead."

"Sure, but why the wait?"

"Amir is coming over in the morning, and we're going to have breakfast. He can drop me off when we're done."

"I think that's great especially since you didn't get a chance to see him yesterday. I know you're down so hopefully he can cheer you up."

"He already has."

"How is that?" my dad stepped forward with a hint of inquisitiveness written on his face.

"Justina is out of her coma. Can you believe it!"

"Are you sure? I spoke to Chantal yesterday and

she didn't mention it."

"It happened this morning. But she's trying to talk so the worse is over."

"This is great news! No wonder you seem like a changed girl. I was so worried about my baby," my mother admitted tearing up as she hugged me again.

"I told you it would all work out." My dad stated as all three of us embraced each other.

"So dad, do you think we can cancel with Pete Anderson today? I want to go for a swim and forget about the case for at least the rest of the day."

"Under the circumstances I think that's a good idea. I'll also inform him about the change in Justina's condition."

"Great. Now all I want is for Justina to make a full recovery. Whoever did this to her and Sway need to pay."

"They will."

"I hope so, daddy, because they didn't deserve that especially Justina. Plus I want this spotlight taken off of me. I don't want fame, especially not this type."

"It'll be over soon. Now go enjoy your swim. I'll see you at the house tomorrow."

"Okay, mom, love you."

"Love you more." We blew each other kisses and I left my mom and dad to say their goodbyes. I couldn't wait to dive into the pool so I could baptize myself and come out with a new beginning.

Unlike yesterday, when I woke up I was beaming.

I couldn't contain the smile on my face and I didn't want to. It seemed like forever since I had anything to smile about. I opened up the drapes on the huge floor length windows and let the sun shine in. After taking a shower I decided to put on an outfit that reflected the awesome born again feeling I had. I opted for a white colored Grecian wrap dress. It had an asymmetric ruffle skirt that fell right above my knees. I accentuated my tiny waist and highlighted my shapely lower body by tightening the self-tie wrap belt. I added my diamond studs and some soft pink shimmery gloss on my lips to finish off my look. I stood in front of the full length mirror to get a full view and I was a vision. As if I was an angel walking right here on earth, which was the exact look I was going for. Since I decided that Amir and I would go out to eat for breakfast, if anybody recognized me, I wanted them to remember me as being the girl who looked like she couldn't hurt a fly. I grabbed my purse and headed downstairs.

As I was walking down the curved staircase my dad was opening the door to let Amir and Genesis in. Amir saw me first and the biggest smile came across his face. I wasn't sure if he would ever look at me that way again but there he was doing just that. "Aaliyah, you look beautiful," Amir grinned as if he couldn't stop himself from saying that even if he wanted to.

"Thank you. I feel amazing this morning."

"I can tell," my dad remarked. "It's wonderful to see my daughter getting back to herself again."

"With that dress on, I guess you decided we won't be eating by the pool."

"I guess," Amir and I both burst out laughing.

"You two enjoy yourselves."

"We will. Bye dad, bye Uncle Genesis," I said giving them both a hug. Amir reached out his hand and I took it as we left.

When Amir opened the front door, it was like we went from one stage of a movie set and was about to step into an entirely different one. The serene morning air was no longer filled with birds chirping and a cool breeze refreshing my face instead there were flashing lights and loud sirens. It seemed like the entire police station had showed up at our front door. Amir held my hand tightly and both my dad and Genesis stood in front of me as if a shield of human protection.

"What do you want?" my dad questioned calmly but his facial expression spoke a different language. It resembled a father who was ready to go to war and had his partner in crime Genesis by his side for the battle.

"This is a warrant to bring Aaliyah Mills Carter back into custody. Her bail has been revoked."

"What!" my voice cracked as the tears began to swell up in my eyes.

"Everything will be fine," Amir whispered in my ear, not letting my hand go.

"Yes, the victim is out of her coma and she has identified Aaliyah Mills as the shooter. Aaliyah Mills please turn around," the police officer ordered pulling out his handcuffs.

"You're lying! Justina would never say that. I didn't shoot her or Sway. This has to be some misunderstanding."

"Please turn around," the officer repeated again completely ignoring my pleas. "Daddy, do something!" I begged as the officer practically ripped my hand away from Amir's to handcuff me.

"I'm calling your attorney right now! Sweetheart, stay strong. I'll fix this." I just shook my head in disbelief. I couldn't believe this was happening to me again. As the officers hauled me off my eyes connected with Amir's. He was completely silent.

"Amir, I didn't do this, please believe me. Pleaaaase." The tears were now pouring down my face. "I love you," I cried out before the officer put me in the back of the squad car and drove off. But my gaze never broke from Amir's until he was completely out of sight.

As I rode in the police car on my way back to being locked up again, this burning sensation that started in the pit of my stomach and shot up to my brain overcame me. The tears instantly stopped flowing from my eyes and I lifted my head up so I was looking straight ahead. I was done with feeling sorry for myself. If it was true that Justina lied to detectives and said I shot her then I vowed to myself to do whatever it took to clear my name even if it meant bringing down my best friend. I wouldn't spend the rest of my life in jail for a crime I didn't commit that I promised myself.

Coming Soon
Boss Bitch

A KING PRODUCTION

Rich
or
Famous

Rich Because You Can Buy Fame

A NOVEL

JOY DEJA KING

Lorenzo

Welcome To My World

Before I die, if you don't remember anything else I ever taught you, know this. A man will be judged, not on what he has but how much of it. So you find a way to make money and when you think you've made enough, make some more, because you'll need it to survive in this cruel world. Money will be the only thing to save you. As I sat across from Darnell those words my father said to me on his deathbed played in my head.

"Yo, Lorenzo, are you listening to me, did you hear anything I said?"

"I heard everything you said. The problem for you is I don't give a fuck." I responded, giving a casual shoulder shrug as I rested my thumb under my chin with my index finger above my mouth.

"What you mean, you don't give a fuck? We been doing business for over three years now and that's the best you got for me?"

"Here's the thing, Darnell, I got informants all over these streets. As a matter of fact that broad you've had in your back pocket for the last few weeks is one of them."

"I don't understand what you saying," Darnell said swallowing hard. He tried to keep the tone of his voice calm, but his body composure was speaking something different.

"Alexus, has earned every dollar I've paid her to fuck wit' yo' blood suckin' ass. You a fake fuck wit' no fangs. You wanna play wit' my 100 g's like you at the casino. That's a real dummy move, Darnell." I could see the sweat beads gathering, resting in the creases of Darnell's forehead.

"Lorenzo, man, I don't know what that bitch told you but none of it is true! I swear 'bout four niggas ran up in my crib last night and took all my shit. Now that I think about it, that trifling ho Alexus probably had me set up! She fucked us both over!"

I shook my head for a few seconds not believing this muthafucker was saying that shit with a straight face. "I thought you said it was two niggas that ran up in your crib now that shit done doubled. Next thing you gon' spit is that all of Marcy projects was in on the stickup."

"Man, I can get your money. I can have it to you first thing tomorrow. I swear!"

"The thing is I need my money right now." I casually stood up from my seat and walked towards Darnell who now looked like he had been dipped in water. Watching him fall apart in front of my eyes made up for the fact that I would never get back a dime of the money he owed me.

"Zo, you so paid, this shit ain't gon' even faze you. All I'm asking for is less than twenty-four hours. You can at least give me that," Darnell pleaded.

"See, that's your first mistake, counting my pockets. My money is *my* money, so yes this shit do faze me."

"I didn't mean it like that. I wasn't tryna disrespect you. By this time tomorrow you will have your money and we can put this shit behind us." Darnell's eyes darted around in every direction instead of looking directly at me. A good liar, he was not.

"Since you were robbed of the money you owe me and the rest of my drugs, how you gon' get me my dough? I mean the way you tell it, they didn't leave you wit' nothin' but yo' dirty draws."

"I'll work it out. Don't even stress yourself, I got you, man."

"What you saying is that the nigga you so called aligned yourself with, by using my money and my product, is going to hand it back over to you?"

"Zo, what you talking 'bout? I ain't aligned myself wit' nobody. That slaw ass bitch Alexus feeding you lies."

"No, that's you feeding me lies. Why don't you admit you no longer wanted to work for me? You felt you was big shit and could be your own boss. So you used my money and product to buy your way in with this other nigga to step in my territory. But you ain't no boss you a poser. And your need to perpetrate a fraud is going to cost you your life."

"Lorenzo, don't do this man! This is all a big misunderstanding. I swear on my daughter I will have your money tomorrow. Fuck, if you let me leave right now I'll have that shit to you tonight!" I listened to Darnell stutter his words.

My men, who had been patiently waiting in each corner of the warehouse, dressed in all black, loaded with nothing but artillery, stepped out of the darkness ready to obliterate the enemy I had once considered my best worker. Darnell's eyes widened as he witnessed the men who had saved and protected him on numerous occasions, as he dealt with the vultures he encountered in the street life, now ready to end his.

"Don't do this, Zo! Pleeease," Darnell was now on his knees begging.

"Damn, nigga, you already a thief and a backstabber.

Don't add, going out crying like a bitch to that too. Man the fuck up. At least take this bullet like a soldier."

"I'm sorry, Zo. Please don't do this. I gotta daughter that need me. Pleeease man, I'll do anything. Just don't kill me." The tears were pouring down Darnell's face and instead of softening me up it just made me even more pissed at his punk ass.

"Save your fuckin' tears. You shoulda thought about your daughter before you stole from me. You're the worse sort of thief. I invite you into my home, I make you a part of my family and you steal from me, you plot against me. Your daughter doesn't need you. You have nothing to teach her."

My men each pulled out their gat ready to attack and I put my hand up motioning them to stop. For the first time since Darnell arrived, a calm gaze spread across his face.

"I knew you didn't have the heart to let them kill me, Zo. We've been through so much together. I mean you Tania's God Father. We bigger than this and we will get through it," Darnell said, halfway smiling as he began getting off his knees and standing up.

"You're right, I don't have the heart to let them kill you, I'ma do that shit myself." Darnell didn't even have a chance to let what I said resonate with him because I just sprayed that muthafucker like the piece of shit he was. "Clean this shit up," I said, stepping over Darnell's bullet ridden body as I made my exit.my exit.

A KING PRODUCTION

DEJA KING

PRESENTS

MAFIA
Princess

A NOVEL

Michelle Monay

Chapter 1
<u>THE SET UP</u>

In the ghetto there are two kinds of street chicks: slut chicks and gutta chicks. If labeled the latter that meant you were on your A-game in the 'hood, fitting Semaj's guise naturally. As she lay snuggled in Gabe's strong arms on the king-sized bed, Semaj smiled inwardly. Gabe was knocked out from the pussy she'd put on him. She glanced at the digital clock atop the nightstand. For the last hour she'd slyly observed the red illuminating numbers change on the dial in anticipation of what was to come.

Just as midnight turned into the one 'o clock hour the sounds of *CLICK-CLACK* startled the light sleeper and for dramatic effect, Semaj screamed fearfully. Instinctively, Gabe went underneath his pillow, and frantically began to search for his weapon. It was an empty space, which he found rather odd. He always slept with his ratchet within reach, but he had realized that he'd left it inside the dresser drawer due to Semaj's persistent request.

"You already know what time it is, fam! Where?" the intruder said calmly as he pointed the barrel of the AK-47 in between the two.

"Where what, man?" Gabe's eyes bugged wide in

shock.

"Don't play with me, son. Fuck is the cash at, my man?"

"I don't keep nothing here, B. Shit's at another spot."

"Now this nigga playing games. It's at another spot, huh?" Mitchell Richardson or Murder Mitch as he was affectionately known in the streets said disbelievingly. "So you gon' keep playin' wit me, nigga?"

"On some real shit, I don't keep shit here, fam." Gabe shrugged his shoulders. "There's nothing in the house, fam."

Mitch's patience was running thin and he was not there to play games. Abruptly the sound of a gun's blast erupted. Mitch had sent a bullet an inch above his head, causing the wood to splinter down the middle. "Don't think you wanna keep playin' around with me, playboy. Take me to the stash." he pressed the hot barrel to Gabe's chest.

Semaj's body shuddered violently as if she was desperately afraid, but the moment she noticed a silhouette in her peripheral view her fright became a serious fear. The moving shadow was approaching with a pistol in hand, and at that instant, Semaj locked eyes with the foreigner. She had to warn her father furtively. "Who is that?" Semaj asked, her heart galloping in uncertainty. Before words could be exchanged, Mitch swiftly shifted his aim. The guy never saw it coming and a slug had been introduced to his head, sending mucus and brain matter spraying throughout the hallway.

"What the fuck?" Gabe roared in devastation. He knew that he was in deep shit.

Mitch had had enough of the bullshit and sliced the side of Gabe's face with the knife on the AK-47, causing it to instantly swell up and bleed. Gabe grunted and winced in excruciating pain. "Now, I know I ain't gotta ask again, my man!" Mitch said calmly. The insane glare in Mitch's eyes was indication that he was itching to let bullets pierce the flesh.

"Shoebox in that closet," Gabe said, willing to give up

his money in trade for Milia's safety. If Milia wasn't involved he would have spit in his face, not giving the stick-up kid the satisfaction of robbing him; he would have died for his no doubt. But more was at stake…Semaj.

"You grab the money for me," Mitch said coldly as he held Gabe at gunpoint and tossed his daughter a knapsack. As instructed, Semaj scuffled over to the closet. She retrieved the money from the Timberland shoebox and a brick of coke that was wrapped in tubes, resembling small fingers. She stuffed the dope and the different denominations into the knapsack.

Semaj handed her father the bagful of goods as he backpedaled out of the room, continuing to have the weapon trained on Gabe. Something told him to put a hot one in him, but it was as if Semaj were speaking through her eyes and nixed the notion.

Easing out of the room, he said threateningly. "Don't move for sixty seconds," Emilio stepped over the fresh corpse as if it was litter on a city street and exited the house.

The daughter and father had accomplished another street robbery, but for some reason an eerie feeling passed over Semaj. A bad feeling. Something in her bones felt wrong, and she wanted nothing more than to get out of there. *Damn we were supposed to play this shit smart not reckless*, she thought. *I ain't know nobody else was even here.*

Gabe wasn't willing to helplessly watch as the stick-up kid got away without an attempt to take his life. Instantly, he popped up and grabbed his .357 chrome Magnum. Semaj held the solemn expression that crossed her face as Gabe left out of the room enraged. He stepped onto the porch, but it was too late. The car was long gone.

Ten minutes later

Gabe hopelessly paced back and forth inside the living room as the human waste was becoming unbearable.

The stench had come from the empty bowels from the dead body and the blood mixture. It wasn't the excessive stink that bothered him though. It was the body, the missing drugs and the money. To owe Gio was to start making funeral arrangements for yourself; not to mention a dead relative. What looked to be a good come-up turned into a bad situation. A very bad situation.

The man had been sent by the notorious Dominican drug boss to deliver him a brick of cocaine via his bowels. The plane had landed that night and he was supposed to do the job, stay overnight and then head back home. Nobody knew that he would no longer be returning. Gabe was hesitant to dial the number he'd been given in case of an emergency. But he knew Gio would find out one way or another, so he manned up and dialed the headman.

"What's the problem, Gabe?" a voice with a thick Dominican accent said.

"Your nephew is dead. Some nigga ran into my spot, but—"

Gio cut him off mid-sentence. "You know I told my family that I could trust you. I vouched for you. Now you are telling me that my family is dead?"

"It's fucked up." Gabe wanted to be apologetic, but with a man like Gio, an apology was no good. He had sent his nephew down out of trust. When that line was broken so was their business relationship and things would only turn deadly.

"You know I have to bury my nephew into the dirt while you remain on earth, Gabe," Gio said as his voice became more aggressive and assertive with each word. "We will meet again, my friend." He hung up.

A piercing scream followed and Gabe's phone collided with the flat screen plasma TV, causing it to split down the center. Gabe threw things around the room violently and fought himself. He frantically grabbed his head and paced the room, fuming. "Word to my Mutha, I'm gonna murder everybody that's associated to the people that set me up! I'ma find out who was behind this shit, son!"

Semaj felt her body temperature rise as her heart began to beat erratically. The sounds of shouting and rattling blared loudly in her ears, sending a twinge up her spine. Her chest became tight as she fidgeted nervously. *I hope I don't look like a suspect,* she thought as her breathing became deep—very deep—panicked.

Finally after his rage subsided, Gabe scuttled into the bedroom. "We gotta get the fuck out of dodge ma! Ain't no tellin' when them slick hair muthafuckas gon' come gunning for my head!" Gabe grabbed as much as he could before they fled from the apartment.

Chapter 2

The club filled quickly as New York's street prestige walked through the door prepared to celebrate the grand opening of Big Pat's strip joint. Everybody who was anybody came out to bring in New Year's Eve with Big Pat and his entourage. A big time hustler, everyone knew who he was. Big Pat and his team were stationed in the glass-skybox that overlooked the club on the third level. Bottles of Cristal and Moet flowed freely at their table as butt naked strippers danced for the 'hood's elite. The VIP area was full of New York's finest and the only people allowed up were the privileged. Big Pat smirked as he sipped his Mo and stood amongst his circle. In New York, Big Pat was like a celebrity. It was his town. Everything about him rang old money too. Dope Money...Dirty Money...Blood Money.

Observing as people poured in, Big Pat focused his attention on the brown-skinned beauty and admired her from afar. Semaj turned heads as she walked through the crowd and he loved how she had instantly stolen his attention. She was definitely the belle of the ball and she had him curious. Semaj's red Prada dress looked as if it were painted on her five feet seven frame, showing off her thick thighs and long legs, and the ostrich thigh high boots made her shine like a rock star in a crowd full of duds. Her hair was pulled high off of her face in a loose ponytail, and her soft baby hair rested flawlessly around her edges. Everything from her eyebrows to her French-pedicured toes was on point and the attention she was getting let her know she had put herself together right.

Envious glares were trained on Semaj as she and Tala made their way up to the bi-level VIP longue. They found a table by the rails, overlooking the live crowd. Semaj could feel the intense stares but she wasn't tripping. She was one breed that women loved to hate. But one thing about Semaj, she knew it and understood why. *If these bitches only knew, I'm not here to try to get their nigga. If anything I'ma hit that stash and send that nigga right back to ya ass,* she laughed inwardly.

"Let me get a glass of Moscato and a bottle of Louie Xlll. The 50 milliliter bottle." Semaj said to the waitress. She ordered the glass just to be extra. Her robbery money was consistent, so she was good and she showed out wherever she went. "It's for all the thirsty bitches lookin' like they wanna fuck a bitch or somethin'." She and Tala shared in laughter.

"Think you mean you'll have a glass of the Louie too. Because the bottle is for five hundred plus." The waitress replied with an attitude.

Semaj wasn't the type of woman that bickered. She simply reached inside her designer clutch purse and pulled out one thousand dollars. Peeling off six hundred dollar bills, all Grants, she said with a cute smirk, "Oh, I'm very sure, babes. Now can you get the Louis and my glass of Moscato?" The waitress didn't even bother to respond and stomped off.

"Why do bitches always seem to be mad? Gotdamn!" Tala exclaimed.

"They ain't comfortable in their own skin. It's just in their damn nature to be angry with the next broad. That's the only explanation I can give for these ratchet ass hoes, auntie." Semaj flung her ponytail. "But I'ma enjoy my birthday. Feel me?" She waited patiently and watched as everyone in VIP got their drink and smoke on.

"Here's *your* glass of Moscato and bottle of *Remy*." The

rude waitress said after finally returning with Semaj's order. She removed an ice-filled bucket from the tray along with her request and placed everything on the table. "That will be $594.00, even," Ms. Attitude said holding her hand out, as if the money wasn't already in front of her.

Semaj snickered, finding the chick comical. She simply picked up the small stack of bills from the table and then smacked the money inside of her sweaty palm. While the waitress counted the money, Semaj popped the cork off the bottle and passed it to Tala.

"And... umm, Big Pat said come up to exclusive VIP. He wanna holla at you," Ms. Attitude spat as her nostrils flared wider with each word spoken.

"Who is Big Pat and what he want with me?" Semaj asked as she wrinkled her brow in confusion.

"Girl, you know exactly who Big Pat is. Don't act like you don't. Please!" she said in annoyance. "Everybody and they momma know that nigga. Don't be cute."

"Sorry, but I'm not everybody and their momma," Semaj retorted.

"I'll make sure to let him know you're *uninterested*."

"Yeah, you do that," Semaj said as Ms. Attitude turned to walk off. "Ay, but sweetie," she called out behind the waitress.

She spun around and thought to herself, *groupie bitch knew she was happy I mentioned Big Pat from jump. Acting all snobbish and shit.* "What 'sup?"

"You forgot my change my dude!" Semaj cracked her face.

She stared at Semaj long faced as though she was speaking foreign language. Tala looked at the waitress, and then back at her niece and burst into a fit of laughter. The shit was too funny. "Bitch you are fuckin' ill, man."

"What? No, I'm not. The broad can act like a bitter

bitch if she like. Bet she won't get a tip from the kid. Not never!"

Digging inside the apron, Ms. Attitude pulled out six crumpled dollar bills. She put them on the table, rolled her eyes snottily and walked off in embarrassment.

"Ay, yo, but did she say that Big Pat wanted you?"

"Right! I wonder what that's about." Semaj said, scanning the club. She knew that the girl was right about her knowing exactly who Big Pat was. Who didn't? He had the streets on lock and ran a very lucrative drug business.

"You know his old, fat ass prolly try'na take you home tonight. You know how they say he do."

"Nigga surely don't want me to be the choice of the night. Nigga won't have a home to come to fuckin' around with me," Semaj joked, but was serious.

"We came out to enjoy ourselves, not searching for potential victims. Damn girl take a night off. Ain't you chillin tonight," Tala stated seriously.

"From the looks dude is checking for me. Right?" Semaj shot. "You know I ain't passing up an opportunity. Feel me?"

"Already know." Tala was too familiar with her niece's intentions and deceitful tactics.

"But watch how I work this stunt though. Schools in session, so take some notes. You just might learn something from the G!" They both cracked up laughing. Subsiding the laughter, Semaj smiled cunningly. She wondered how the game would play itself out tonight.

The girls sat modestly as they watched the crowd grow thicker and they partied like socialites. It was just a little after midnight and unsurprisingly the club had reached its capacity. At that moment, Semaj noticed her father cashing security out for admission. "Mitch's ass always lurking," Tala said as she spotted Semaj's father easing his way into a booth in the corner. He was so far back that he was almost hidden by the shadows of the abandoned section of the club. All of the other partygoers were crowded around the stage while Mitch was scoping out the scene, trying to be as inconspicuous as possible.

Just then a tall dark skinned guy approached them. "Ay, mami in the red. My boy said come holla at 'im up in the top VIP."

"Names not mami. But if your *boy* wanna holla at me," she pointed her forefinger at herself and then at him, "why is he sending you to do his job? What you his spokesman or some shit?"

"Nah," he sucked his teeth. "It ain't shit like that, ma. He just up in exclusive VIP. He ain't try'na get tackled coming down here and shit. It's Big Pat. You know how that shit be. We move different from the average nigga, baby girl."

"Knows nothing about that, my man. But this what you can do for me. Tell your boy if he try'na get at me, he know where I am. There's no need to send other niggas. We all grown here. I'll be here for a li'l while longer though," she faked a huge smile.

"Dammmmn! You just cut like that huh, ma? I see you got ya swag thang going," he laughed, finding her rare response amusing. "But I'ma be sure to tell the nigga what's up."

"You do that," Semaj said as he turned to walk off.

"Nigga just don't know he walkin' his self into a fuckin' fucked-up trap. Stupid niggas a holla at anybody with a pretty face." Tala shook her head. She'd seen it all one too many times.

"Don't hate," Semaj laughed. "This my shit right here TaTa." She perched up. With the bottle in her hand, Semaj graciously moved back and forth to the hip-hop tunes. It was cute how Semaj was so gorgeous as if she stepped out of a Cosmopolitan magazine, but was bopping to Gucci Mane as though she was nothing but street, and street she was.

"Kick a door nigga... kick a door nigga... everybody... everybody on the floor nigga," she chuckled, chanting along to the lyrics. *"On the low dawg... I'm cutthroat, nigga... "* Semaj hoodishly but femininely grooved to the beat.

"Damn, I really had to travel all the way down here huh, ma?" a male voice behind her said. Already knowing it had to be the infamous Big Pat, she decided to immediately put her plan into motion. Playing a role, Semaj quickly glanced back at him and replied, "I mean it was your choice." She stepped a foot forward as if she was uninterested. Semaj knew trying to play the hard-to-get role was dicey, but she didn't care because in most cases it was the payoff.

Big Pat chuckled, knowing she couldn't know who he was. "And that's not often for a man of my caliber ma," Big Pat whispered in her ear smugly. "Why don't you come and chill with me and my peoples in VIP? It's exclusively for us. It's my birthday, so we doin' it real big up top."

"How ironic. It's my birthday also," Semaj continued to slowly sway her mid-section as she overlooked the dense horde.

"How old you turn?" he asked with a charming smile.

"I'm twenty-two," she responded.

"That's what's up. Come up and kick it with me and my entourage. It's a celebration"

"Thanks for the offer, but I'm no groupie. I'm good." Semaj still was throwing shade and had barely given him any face. She was half-glancing him to death and placed her attention back to the animated crowd below her.

"I can tell that, ma. And that's what I like about you. So can I get a name?"

"And why do you want my name? Big Pat is it?" She questioned, her Brooklyn accent rolling off thick. "You can get at any girl in here I'm sure. Being that you have spokespeople that extol just something as simple as your name. I assume you are the man around here."

He laughed at her as he rubbed his goatee. "I see you an ole comedian or something, ma. You got jokes."

"Seriously. You got people coming down here like I was 'pose to know you. Who are you really?" Semaj questioned, glancing back at him.

"Patrick is my name. Yours?" He gently grabbed her arm and turned her around to face him.

"Now that's much better and more attention capturing." It was now game time. Time to seem interested. "Nice to meet you Patrick. My name is Ashley." Semaj decided to go with her gut instinct and gave him a fake name. "Now what is it that you want with me?"

"Everything," he replied.

"Everything?"

"Come chill with me up top li'l one. We can discuss more up there."

"Nah, me and my girl was fenna bounce in a few minutes. I gotta go to work in the morning," she lied, but it was all a part of her plan.

"Why somebody as fine as you doing working ma?" Big Pat asked. "See, if you was with a nigga like me you wouldn't know what it felt like to work, ma."

"That's corny bum shit," she shot with a smirk. "And for the record, I'm independent. I make my own paper, baby."

"Damn! I respect that shit," Big Pat grinned, finding this woman to be a piece of work. Running the streets he had dealt with all sorts of women but it was just something different about this one right here. Something intriguing. "Why don't you leave with me tonight? I'll make up for your paycheck."

"Sorry. Not a one-nightstander or none of that, babes. I'm not into going to hotels, traps, or none of that desperate shit. For a guy of your supposedly caliber," Semaj said sarcastically. "You just pick random girls up at the club frequently?" she asked, eyebrow furrowed in curiosity.

"I see you just gon' give me a hard time."

"No doubt. What you thought I was going to be easy?"

"Nah. Fo'real, I done already deciphered your persona. You rare, I can admit that. So going to the hotel and one-nighting you ain't happening. Where I lay my head comfortably is where you'll be. Trust. So you leavin' with me?" he asked confidently.

"Sorry, but I don't leave the club with dudes that I don't know. That's not my *persona* either," she stated as she shifted all her weight on one leg, giving her hips an enticing shape. Semaj was a professional in this area of studies, and knew she had dude right where she wanted him to be. If the streets required a degree, she'd already graduated summa cum laude. "I'll give you my number though. Maybe when I get off work tomorrow we can go out somewhere. That's if that's cool with you, you know."

Big Pat stared at her intensely. He was astounded. Semaj was really holding her own. Her traits were of a woman that held respect for herself. One that he could consider to court. She appeared harmless, lovable... innocent but in actuality, all Semaj knew was harm and she had lost her innocence as a child. It was a shame what the world had turned her into. She was a con artist and a very manipulative woman. She was untrustworthy and had been for a very long time.

"No doubt, ma. I'm feelin' that," he pulled out his BlackBerry and handed it to her. She stored her number and handed the phone back to him. "I'ma get up wit' you tomorrow evening some time."

Semaj graciously nodded her head as she said, "C'mon, Tala." Semaj purposely set the half of bottle of Remy atop the table. She walked out of the VIP lounge and down the wraparound stairs. Big Pat watched from the railing as she left the building, just as she knew he would. *I got him,* she thought silently as she exited the club all the while texting her father their next potential victim. Little did Semaj know that her encounter with Big Pat would have an impact on her life forever.

A King Production
Order Form

A King Production
P.O. Box 310367
Jamaica, NY 11431
www.joykingonline.com
www.twitter.com/joydejaking

Name: _____

Address: _____

City/State: _____

Zip: _____

QUANTITY	TITLES	PRICE	TOTAL
_____	Bitch	$15.00	_____
_____	Bitch Reloaded	$15.00	_____
_____	The Bitch Is Back	$15.00	_____
_____	Queen Bitch	$15.00	_____
_____	Last Bitch Standing	$15.00	_____
_____	Bitch Chronicles	$25.00	_____
_____	Superstar	$15.00	_____
_____	Ride Wit' Me	$12.00	_____
_____	Stackin' Paper	$15.00	_____
_____	Trife Life To Lavish	$15.00	_____
_____	Trife Life To Lavish II	$15.00	_____
_____	Stackin' Paper II	$15.00	_____
_____	Rich or Famous	$15.00	_____
_____	Bitch A New Beginning	$15.00	_____
_____	Princess Fever "Birtday Bash"	$9.99	_____

Shipping/Handling (Via Priority Mail) $5.50 1-2 Books, $7.95 3-4 Books add $1.95 for ea. Additional book.

Total: $_____ **FORMS OF ACCEPTED PAYMENTS:** Certified or government issued checks and money Orders, all mail in orders take 5-7 Business days to be delivered.

Joy (Deja) King

About the Author

Deja (Joy) King was born in Toledo, Ohio, and raised in California, Maryland, North Carolina and New Jersey. Ms. King represents a new breed of writers producing young, hip and sexy novels that introduce readers to street life in all its complexity and also takes readers behind the velvet rope of the glamorous, but often shady entertainment industry.

Ms. King attended North Carolina Central University and Pace University, where she majored in journalism. Emerging onto the entertainment scene, Deja accepted an internship position, and immediately began to work her way up the ranks, at The Terrie Williams Agency. She worked hands-on with Johnnie Cochran, The Essence Awards, The Essence Music Festival, The

NBA Players' Association, Moet & Chandon, and other entertainment executives and celebrities.

Following a new chapter in her life, Ms. King attended the Lee Strasburg Theater Institute before accepting a job as Director of Hip Hop Artist Relations at Click Radio, where she developed segments featuring the biggest names in hip hop. Ms. King pushed her department to new levels by creating an outlet that placed hip hop in the forefront of the cyber world.

Ms. King made her literary debut with *Bitch*, and followed it up with the bestselling sequel *Bitch Reloaded* and *The Bitch Is Back*. The saga continues with *Queen Bitch*. A prolific writer, King is also the author of *Dirty Little Secrets*, *Hooker to Housewife*, *Superstar*, *Stackin' Paper*, *Trife Life To Lavish* and *Stackin' Paper 2 Genesis' Payback* which she writes under her pseudonym Joy King.

For more information visit www.joykingonline.com
www.twitter.com/joydejaking
Follow me on facebook
"JoyDejaKing" fan page

COMING
Oct. 2011

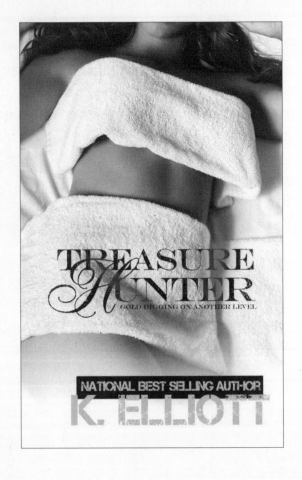

TREASURE HUNTER
GOLD DIGGING ON ANOTHER LEVEL

NATIONAL BEST SELLING AUTHOR
K. ELLIOTT